THE SECRET
DAKOTA

#2 The Haunted City of Gold

Jake MacKenzie

SCHOLASTIC INC.
New York Toronto London Auckland Sydney

Design and Illustration: **Hal Aber**

Cover Illustration: **Bill Purdom**

Photographs: **Neal Edwards**

Scholastic Books are available at special discounts for quantity purchases for use as premiums, promotional items, retail sales through specialty market outlets, etc. For details contact: Special Sales Manager, Scholastic Inc., 730 Broadway, New York, NY 10003.

ISBN 0-590-40750-3

12 11 10 9 8 7 6 5 4 3 2 1   7 8 9/8 0 1 2/9
                                                 11

Printed in the U.S.A.
First Scholastic printing, November 1987

Hi Boss!

Please excuse the mess. I had to make sure you knew this was really from me, so I made a thumbprint. Had an interesting experience in the jungle, as you'll see from the file of stuff I left you. If you move fast, you can grab the thief yourself. He'll be in the United States in the next few weeks.

So why don't you get together with the agents in the Z.O.O., pick through the clues here in THE HAUNTED CITY OF GOLD file, and decide who the criminal really is? (By the way, don't worry about the guy who delivered this. He's an aquaintance of mine from my jungle adventures.)

Heard an interesting rumor about some smugglers. I want to check it out. Then I'm due for a vacation. Maybe a little bike trip, who knows?

I'm outta here, Boss!

DK

ZONE OPERATIONS ORGANIZATION
9009 Incognito Drive Arlington, Virginia 90909
703·555·9009   TELEX: 99-9009

MEMORANDUM

TO: All agents in the Z.O.O. (Zone Operations
Organization)
FROM: The Zookeeper
CONCERNING: The Dakota King File

THE HAUNTED CITY OF GOLD

There was a knock at my door at midnight. I opened
it just in time to see a barefoot man in some kind of
native costume go running off down the street. On my
doorstep was a small suitcase made of woven straw
with Dakota King's note.

When I opened the straw suitcase I found the usual
mess: transcripts of conversations King recorded with
his little wrist recorder, photographs, drawings,
notes, maps, scraps of papers, all kinds of odds and
ends. Dakota King and his associate, Longh Gonh,
always do the same thing: gather up the clues and
leave the mystery solving to me . . . and to you agents.

If Dakota and Longh were still Z.O.O. agents instead

of Disappearing Inc. freelance adventurers, believe me I would keep them in line. None of this crazy file business. But Dakota never was one for doing the dull work. Disappearing Inc. is a good name for an agency run by a guy like that.

Meanwhile, of course, we've got to sift through this mess and see what these two have uncovered for us this time. Since I don't have time to work on this myself, I'm sending copies of what Dakota left with me to all Z.O.O. agents. THAT MEANS YOU! Copies of everything are here. What I want you to do is read it all and figure out who committed the crime.

I've attached Dakota's note, his profile, and my instructions in the file which follows.

Good luck, agents. You'll need it.

The Zookeeper

Zone Operations Organization

CONFIDENTIAL PROFILE REPORT

Subject: Dakota King
Age: Unrecorded
Height: 6′ 3″
Distinguishing marks: Eagle tattoo on inside of left wrist
Address: General Post Office Every Major City
Home Base: Redd Cliff, Colorado
Contact Base: The Z.O.O.
Partner and Contact: Longh Gonh (separate profile on file), Disappearing Inc. agent
Occupation: Agent-at-large for own agency, Disappearing Inc.
Services valued by Organization: Investigative skills used in studies of unexplained events, uncharted territories, unsolved mysteries of the world.
Special Interests: Freedom and justice for all—especially Dakota King; fine art and illustration (published works of Dakota King's own art include: Dakota King's Sketchbook, King's Ransom: Collected Drawings of Dakota King, and Dakota!); magic (King is a world-renowned magician known for contributing

numerous tricks and illusions to master magicians on all continents).

Education: Life experience. Spent boyhood traveling with anthropologist parents who found him living with the Kayuga Indians in Death Valley and adopted him when he was a small boy. Travels exposed him to numerous tribal cultures in this country and all over the world.

While living with the Kayuga he received survival training, learned to read nature's danger signals, learned to use the celestial bodies, the oceans, rivers, and earth's vibrations as means of predicting events and even changing events. Acclaimed expert in the customs and mystical ceremonies of American Indian tribes. Followed and lived with Gypsy tribes in Hungary, Italy, and throughout Europe. Accepted and welcomed by all Gypsy tribes on every continent as adopted son of Zolan, King of the Gypsies. No stranger to the Himalayas and the unnumbered villages and unchartered regions which lay hidden on the summits, in the valleys, and in the caves of these mysterious mountains. Recognized expert in knowledge of great impostors of the 18th, 19th, and 20th centuries.

Experience: Consultant to government intelligence agencies in the use of illusions for diversion tactics to be used as alternatives to weapons. References available on request from members of the private sector who have used his services for finding lost treasures and tracing family fortunes.

Hobbies: Flying, race car driving, D & D, art, inventing communication devices, and experiencing life.

ROCKET RESEARCH LABORATORY

2731 CROSSTIMBERS ROAD   HOUSTON, TX 77093

TO: Professor Bricknow, Leland University
FROM: Rocket Research Lab, Special Projects
RE: Strange Satellite Sighting

On its 254th orbit around the Earth, our super-secret big eye satellite found an unusual infrared pattern in the jungles of South America.

Preliminary readings suggest the ruins of an ancient city, possibly the city of Lanera, known in legend as the Haunted City of Gold.

There is a mummy in the storage room at the Museum of Prehistory in Paramar. Around its neck is a gold medallion whose inscription shows where the secret wealth of Lanera is hidden. What we would like you to do is go to Paramar, examine the medallion, then search for the treasure. It is of vital importance to a top secret government project that you do this. If our guess is correct, there is a special metal there which we need for our work. One of our agents will be in touch with you to explain in person the grave importance of the mission.

Please treat this message with the utmost urgency and secrecy. We await your reply.

LELAND UNIVERSITY

135 RUSSELL MILLS ROAD   NEW BEDFORD, MA 02748

MEMORANDUM

TO: Rocket Research Laboratory, Special Projects
FROM: Professor Bricknow, Leland Univerity
RE: Strange Satellite Sightings

I agree. Your pictures do show what may well be
the ancient city of Lanera. Unfortunately, I will not
be able to go for you. I am still sick with malaria and
would not last a day in the jungle. So I have asked
Dakota King, the son of a colleague who is a professor
of anthropology, to go in my place. Mr. King and his
companion, Longh Gonh, are more than capable of
doing the job. With your permission, I will pass all
information on to them.

I have complete trust in Dakota King and will send
him a sealed explanation of the purpose of his
mission. He will be instructed to open the envelope
only when and if he locates the legendary "golden
wealth" of Lanera. Should he fail in his mission,
which I doubt, he need never know of the true reason
for the search.

Dakota King's
Microdiary Entry #1
Re: The Haunted City of Gold

It was a hot, dusty bus ride to the jungle town of Paramar. Longh and I arrived with a bunch of tourists to avoid suspicion. If word got out that we were here on a government mission we <u>might</u> get a little more attention than we wanted. I had known Professor Bricknow since I was a boy. When he was at the same university as my father, he was the one who taught me how to interpret many ancient carvings and symbols. Knowing how much trust he had in me, I was not even tempted to break the seal of the envelope he had entrusted to me until I reached the Haunted City of Gold. I turned off any curiosity I had and thought of the task ahead of me.

In preparation for our mission, I checked our supplies—my microrecorder watch was all set with new miniature disks and a fresh pack of solar-powered batteries. As you know, Boss, ever since I invented this little gizmo, I leave my notebooks at home. I just click on the little gadget, and it takes down what I want. I had also brought along my portable computer. You never know when you might need data, even in a jungle. My art supplies were packed, too. I'd given my belt-buckle camera such a workout on that last adventure with the snakes that I wore out the advance on it. Good thing I have a photographic memory, Boss. I'll just have to rely on that and my sketching skills. So get ready for some pretty pictures. Naturally, I packed a few candy bars just in case I couldn't get a hamburger around here. A guy's gotta eat. Longh, of course, was probably looking forward to a diet of banana leaves and insects.

When he and I reached Paramar, we checked into our small hotel, unpacked, then made our way to the Museum of Prehistory. On Professor Bricknow's instructions, we were to ask for an archaeologist by the name of Henry Wallach. He was supposed to show Longh and me the mummy of the Laneran boy king and his medallion.

The museum was a great, dark, and gloomy place on a narrow side street. As instructed, we went to the side entrance. I pressed a door buzzer and a tall, skinny man with large watery eyes answered the door.

We said we had been sent by Professor Bricknow. The man simply nodded and let us in. He acted strangely, not even introducing himself, though he nodded slightly when we asked if he was Wallach.

I switched on my microrecorder just in case he was going to say anything more than: "This way to the mummy."

****

TRANSCRIPT

DK: Did you receive Professor Bricknow's wire?

WALLACH: Yes, it just arrived yesterday. Tell me what I can do to help.

DK: First we'd like to see the mummy of the boy king.

WALLACH: Yes, of course. Follow me, please. Do you know the story about him?

DK: Just that he was the last ruler of some mysterious city.

WALLACH: That's part of it. Legends tell of a civilization that flourished in the jungle for thousands of years. Until about thirty years ago, that's all it was—a legend. Then some prospectors found this mummy and gave him to our museum. Archaeologists excavated his tomb. According to some scrolls buried with him, there were many kings and queens who ruled the civilization over the centuries. When each king or queen died, the people buried their ruler in a graveyard that was an exact replica of their own capital city.

DK: And that's where he was found?

WALLACH: No. The boy was buried in a plain stone grave high in the mountains. It was not the grand tomb of a king. No other tombs were anywhere in sight.

As near as we can deduce from the scrolls, the boy's parents died shortly after he was born. The high priests took this to be a bad omen. The boy, who was the last of the line of rulers, became deathly ill. At about the same time, a nearby volcano began to smoke and heat up. As the boy got sicker, the volcano got hotter.

The high priests of the country had a meeting, decided a great catastrophe was about to happen, and that something must be done. They had the people gather up what the scrolls called their "golden wealth" and hid it. We think it was buried somewhere in the city of

THE DEAD KINGS AND QUEENS, THE HAUNTED CITY OF GOLD.

LONGH GONH: WHAT WAS THIS WEALTH: GOLD BARS? JEWELRY?

WALLACH: WE DON'T REALLY KNOW. THE CITIZENS OF LANERA DIDN'T DO MUCH MINING THAT WE KNOW OF. NO ONE HAS EVER FOUND MUCH IN THE WAY OF GOLD MINES IN THESE JUNGLES, BUT THAT DOESN'T MEAN THEY DON'T EXIST. THE LANERANS LIVED IN THE JUNGLES FOR TWELVE THOUSAND YEARS. THEY MAY WELL HAVE HAD SECRET GOLD MINES AT SOME TIME DURING THAT LONG PERIOD.

DK: WHAT HAPPENED TO EVERYONE?

WALLACH: THE HIGH PRIESTS WERE RIGHT ABOUT THE CATASTROPHE. THE VOLCANO ERUPTED AND BURIED THE ANCIENT CITY FOR CENTURIES—ARCHAEOLOGISTS ONLY DISCOVERED IT A FEW YEARS AGO, AFTER THE BOY KING'S TOMB WAS FOUND. HOWEVER, THE GRAVEYARD REPLICA OF THE CITY STILL REMAINS BURIED IN THE JUNGLE. WE HAVE FOUND NO "GOLDEN WEALTH," NO SIGN OF THE GRAND TOMBS. DO NOT BE MISLED BY THAT TOURIST TRAP OF A PHONY RUINED CITY. [TOURIST TRAP IS RIGHT, BOSS— LONGH AND I HAD SEEN SIGNS ALL OVER PARAMAR FOR LOST CITY THIS AND LOST CITY THAT.] THE TRUE CITY HAS ONLY BEEN SEEN BY A FEW ARCHAEOLOGISTS. ITS BURIAL GROUND REPLICA HAS BEEN SEEN BY NO ONE. BOTH CITIES REMAIN OUT OF REACH TO THE CASUAL TOURIST, NO MATTER WHAT THE HUCKSTERS IN PARAMAR SAY.

LG: HAS ANYONE CHECKED THE AREA WHERE THE BOY WAS FOUND?

WALLACH: OH YES. LONG AND HARD, BUT NO ONE FOUND ANYTHING. WE NOW THINK THE LANERAN PRIESTS DELIBERATELY BURIED THE BOY AWAY FROM THE TOMBS OF THE OTHERS.

DK: WHY?

WALLACH: BECAUSE, AS YOU'LL SEE, HE IS WEARING A GOLD MEDALLION. ON IT IS INSCRIBED A DRAWING, WHICH LEGEND SAYS IS THE KEY TO FINDING THE GOLDEN WEALTH. THE PRIESTS WANTED TO KEEP IT SEPARATE FROM THE PLACE WHERE THE WEALTH WAS HIDDEN TO MAKE IT HARDER FOR GRAVE ROBBERS.

THE IDEA WORKED. UNTIL RECENTLY NOBODY HAD ANY IDEA WHERE THE HAUNTED CITY OF GOLD WAS, SO THE INSCRIPTION ON THE MEDALLION HAS BEEN USELESS. [WE CONTINUED WALKING TOWARD THE BACK OF THE MUSEUM. THERE, IN THE GLASS CASE, WAS A MUMMY OF A SMALL INDIAN BOY. THE THREE OF US STOOD THERE SILENTLY. WALLACH BROKE THE SILENCE.] THERE [HE WHISPERED AS HE POINTED] IS THE MEDALLION.

END OF TRANSCRIPT

****

A phone rang in a distant part of the museum. Since no one was around at the time, Wallach went off to answer it. While he was gone, I stepped in front of the case and studied the medallion design, which I later drew from memory.

When Wallach returned, we told him about the satellite photos we'd brought showing what might be the location of the Haunted City of Gold. His eyes instantly looked less watery and a lot sharper. He asked if we could leave them with him **to study overnight.** I agreed, knowing he was Bricknow's trusted contact in Paramar. But I told him he could only have the photos overnight. Also, I gave him copies, not the originals, and they're too blurry to use as any kind of guide. I never completely trust anyone I haven't met before.

Longh and I left, satisfied that the first stage of our job had gone so smoothly.

CLUE #1

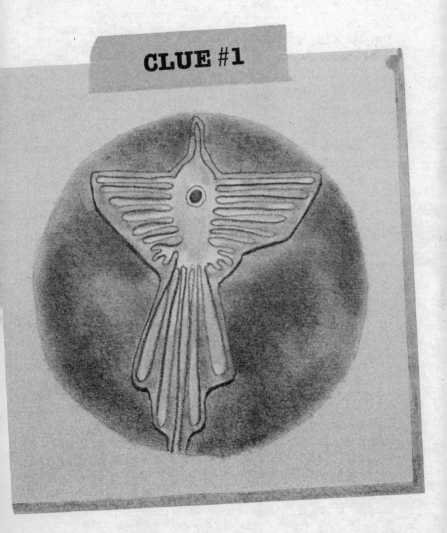

Dakota King's
Microdiary Entry #2
Re: The Haunted City of Gold

Later that evening Longh and I found a small outdoor restaurant in Paramar where we decided to have
our dinner. It was pleasant sitting outside. There was
still some light, and the heat of the day was fading.

As we waited for our food to come, Longh confessed
something to me. "You know, Dakota, there is something about Wallach that concerns me—his immediate
and intense interest in those photographs. Perhaps
they aroused only his professional archaeological interest, perhaps something more."

"I agree, Longh. But Professor Bricknow trusts
him, and I guess we'll have to as well. Besides, the pictures I gave him are too muddy to be useful unless he
has other information. We will surely find the Haunted
City before anyone else."

"Silence, Dakota."

He was right. Anyone could be listening. I looked
around me. The restaurant wasn't very crowded. At
one table were an older man and woman, at another
two local people talking to each other, and at a third a
bearded man wearing dark glasses while reading the
newspaper.

"Even in the usual, there is the strange," my Ninja
master once told me. There was definitely something

strange about the man. At first I couldn't put my finger on what it was, but then I figured it out. He hadn't turned a page in a long time. Either he was a slow reader, or he had something else on his mind. I deliberately stared at him. He raised the paper in front of his face. As he did I noticed something else. **The tip of the index finger on his right hand was missing.**

I was about to mention this to Longh when a small group of musicians came strolling by, followed by a crowd of dancing people in brightly colored costumes.

"A local festival, Señor," the waiter explained to us as he served our food.

I sat there, pretending to watch the parade and enjoy the music. Suddenly, from that direction, something whizzed past my face, so close it brushed against my cheek. I heard the thunk of something hitting the wall behind my right ear. When I put my fingertips to my face, I saw blood on them.

Stuck in a wooden post behind my head was a small double-edged dagger. A thin layer of blood, my blood, was on one edge of the blade. We jumped up to chase the strolling players, but by that time they had disappeared into the back streets of the town.

Returning to our table, I pulled out my handkerchief and held it to my face with one hand. With the other I yanked the dagger out of the post. There was a strip of thick paper wrapped around the handle.

"Why can't they use the telephone like everyone else?" I said, touching my stinging cut. "What ring is he talking about?"

"Perhaps," said Longh, peeling away some colored crêpe paper from the handle of the dagger, "this ring." And there, under the paper, was a gold ring. I slipped it off the dagger and examined it more closely. It was a plain gold ring, flattened on one side. On the flat part was an engraving of a strange-looking bird, identical to the one on the medallion of the boy king.

CLUE #2

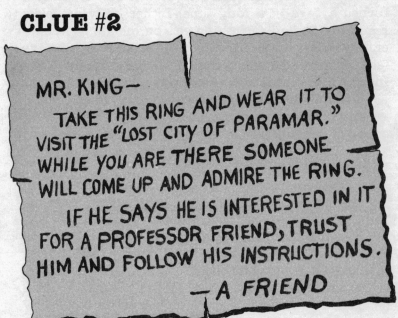

MR. KING—
TAKE THIS RING AND WEAR IT TO VISIT THE "LOST CITY OF PARAMAR."
WHILE YOU ARE THERE SOMEONE WILL COME UP AND ADMIRE THE RING.
IF HE SAYS HE IS INTERESTED IN IT FOR A PROFESSOR FRIEND, TRUST HIM AND FOLLOW HIS INSTRUCTIONS.
—A FRIEND

Just then I had a thought. I looked for the man with the newspaper. He was gone. When the waiter came by, I asked for some ice water for my cut.

"What happened, Señor?" he asked.

"One of your local fun-lovers got carried away," I joked. When he came back with the water, Longh asked how we could get to the Lost City of Paramar.

"If you are interested, my brother will take you there tomorrow in his taxi," the waiter said. "There he is, parked on the other side of the village square." He waved to a man slouching against a beat-up cab.

"It could prove most instructive," said Longh, eyeing the cab. "After all, we are just tourists."

Dakota King's
Microdiary Entry #3
Re: The Haunted City of Gold

The following morning found us bumping our way toward one of the biggest tourist traps in Central America. Every fifty feet there was a sign with big red letters: LOST CITY THIS WAY! or TWO MILES TO THE LOST CITY OF PARAMAR!

As the cab skidded around the curve, we finally saw it: a big gate with a curved sign over it that read: GO NO FARTHER! THIS IS IT! WELCOME TO THE LOST CITY!

"Can you tell me something?" Longh asked the cabdriver. "Why do you call this a lost city? It does not seem particularly hard to find."

"Oh, it's never really been lost, but how many people would want to come to a found city?" the cabdriver asked. "The story I heard is that a long time ago some American archaeologists wandered through here. They went down the road and found all these stones. When they came out of the trees, they claimed they had discovered a lost civilization.

"Well, that was news to us—we had known about the place for years. But once all the tourists came here to see it, we agreed that, yes indeed, it was a lost city. Especially when we saw how much money we could make," he said. Longh and I got out of the cab by the

Lost City Cafe and walked by the Lost City Souvenir Shop to take a tour.

It wasn't much of a city. Just a pile of old rocks here and there. It was hard to tell what any of these buildings were, but it didn't matter. The guide just seemed to make it up as he went along. This pile of stone was an ancient temple. That pile of stone was an altar for human sacrifice. And so on. He had a good imagination.

At the end of the tour he asked if there were any questions. I raised my hand and asked if this place was related to Lanera and the Haunted City of Gold. The guide looked a little annoyed and simply said, "There is no such place, Señor! This is the only ancient city in our country."

The so-called tour broke up shortly afterwards. One man hung back from the departing crowd and walked toward me. He was short, had bright dark eyes, jet black hair, and a blue smudge on his left earlobe. As he got closer I realized it was a tiny tattoo. Of a bird. The bird. The man began to speak. I slipped the gold ring on my finger and flicked on my microrecorder watch.

****

TRANSCRIPT

MAN: Excuse me, Señor.

DK: Yes.

MAN: My name is Ortega. I am an amateur archaeologist, and I overheard your question about the Haunted City of Gold. Are you an archaeologist as well?

DK: No, just a curious tourist who happened to read about the city

IN A GUIDEBOOK. I TAKE IT YOU'RE INTERESTED IN THE SUBJECT.

ORTEGA: YES. IT IS SOMETHING OF A HOBBY OF MINE. YOU SEE, I BELONG TO THE ORDER OF THE PHOENIX. THE PHOENIX, AS YOU PROBABLY KNOW, SEÑOR, IS A MYTHICAL BIRD BELIEVED TO HAVE RISEN FROM ITS ASHES AFTER BEING BURNED. AND SO THE EMBLEM OF OUR ORDER IS A FEATHERED BIRD. [HE POINTED TO THE TATTOO ON HIS EARLOBE.] WE ARE A GROUP WHO BELIEVE WE ARE DESCENDED FROM THE LANERANS. WE ALSO BELIEVE WE ARE ENTITLED TO WHAT THEY LEFT BEHIND AND, LIKE THE PHOENIX, WE WILL RISE AGAIN AS A PEOPLE. FOR YEARS NOW WE HAVE BEEN LOOKING FOR THE RESTING PLACE OF OUR KINGS AND QUEENS.

DK: THAT'S ALL VERY INTERESTING, MR. ORTEGA, BUT WHY ARE YOU TELLING ME THIS?

ORTEGA: BECAUSE, SEÑOR, YOU SEEMED SO CURIOUS ABOUT THE SUBJECT...AND BECAUSE I NOTICED YOUR UNUSUAL RING. TELL, ME, WOULD YOU CONSIDER SELLING IT?

DK: WHY DO YOU ASK?

ORTEGA: A FRIEND OF MINE, A PROFESSOR [HE PAUSED AND LOOKED STRAIGHT INTO MY EYES], OWNED ONE VERY MUCH LIKE IT. I PROMISED THAT IF I EVER SAW ANOTHER ONE I WOULD TRY AND GET IT FOR HIM.

DK: I MIGHT CONSIDER IT AT THE RIGHT PRICE. RIGHT NOW I'M RELUCTANT TO LET IT GO BECAUSE I ACQUIRED IT SO, UH, RECENTLY.

ORTEGA: VERY WELL. THINK IT OVER. LET ME GIVE YOU MY CARD. IF YOU CHANGE YOUR MIND, YOU MAY CONTACT ME. GOOD DAY, SEÑOR.

END OF TRANSCRIPT

****

Well, Boss, he gave me an ordinary-looking business card and walked away. I turned to Longh and said, "How do you like that? I guess that wasn't our guy after all."

"Do not be so sure, Dakota. Look on the other side of the card," Longh instructed.

I turned it over and found this note and small map.

CLUE #3

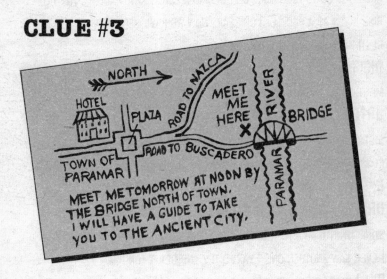

That afternoon we returned to our hotel, and there was a telegram waiting for us.

CLUE #4

Telegram

western union

	DATE	FILING TIME
	5/5	8:18 AM

ORIGINATING OFFICE > U.S.A.

MESSAGE NUMBER > 0023

TO: DAKOTA KING

ADDRESS: LOST CITY HOTEL

CITY — STATE & ZIP CODE: PARAMAR

DAKOTA--

CALL ME AT THE UNIVERSITY SCIENCE CENTER.

AUNT ELIZA

SIGNED: *Eliza King*

Dakota King's
Microdiary Entry #4
Re: The Haunted City of Gold

"I think someone is playing a little joke," said Longh when I showed him the telegram. "You don't have an aunt named Eliza."

"I know," I said. "It's a code I worked out with my computer genius, Zan.'

"You mean Alexandra?" Longh said. Zan was her code name. Mine was Tarzan.

"The very one. When we get up to the room, I'll give her a call."

As we approached the door of our room, Longh stopped and pointed to the top edge of the door. Each time we left the room, one of us pulled a hair from his head and closed the door on it. If the hair was still there when we returned, that meant no one had paid a surprise visit to our room. If the hair was gone, someone had been in the room, and the intruder might still be there. This time the hair was gone! Slowly and silently, Longh turned the doorknob and, in a flash, threw open the door. We both jumped in, ready for an attack, but no one was there. Everything looked undisturbed, but a large basket of fruit had been delivered while we were gone.

"Room service!" I said in disgust. Hate to waste the old adrenaline.

Longh went over to the basket and picked up the card. "A gift from the museum."

Longh pulled off the plastic covering on the fruit and took out a fresh mango. "Have one, Dakota. A healthy diet is important in preparing us for the jungle rigors ahead."

"No thanks, Longh," I said, reaching deep into my backpack for the stash of chocolate bars I'd picked up back at the American airport. "I'm going to see what kind of message Aunt Eliza left for us."

I set up my portable computer and connected my special communications equipment to it. In a few minutes I was hooked into my telephone line to Zan's computer at the university. I typed in our special code— a series of seven flower-like computer symbols representing the days of the week. I left off the third bud, which represented Tuesday, the day I was calling.

$$\overset{\displaystyle *}{!}\;\overset{\displaystyle *}{!}\;\overset{\displaystyle }{!}\;\overset{\displaystyle *}{!}\;\overset{\displaystyle *}{!}\;\overset{\displaystyle *}{!}\;\overset{\displaystyle *}{!}$$

In no time my computer began whirring, recording the information Zan had for me. After the transmission was over, I hung up the phone and played the message back across my computer screen.

COMPUTER CONVERSATION

● HIYA HONEY! HOW'S THE JUNGLE? DO YOU GET FREE BANANAS AND PINEAPPLES?

● WHAT HAVE YOU GOT FOR ME, ZAN?

● GOT A MESSAGE FOR YOU FROM PRO-
FESSOR BRICKNOW. SAYS HE'S SORRY TO
HAVE SENT YOU ON A WILD GOOSE CHASE. BY
NOW YOU KNOW THAT MR. WALLACH IS NOT AT
THE PARAMAR MUSEUM. HE IS VISITING HERE
AT THE UNIVERSITY. HE SAYS IT WILL BE A
WHILE BEFORE HE GETS BACK TO PARAMAR,
SO YOU MIGHT WANT TO COME HOME AND
TALK TO HIM HERE. WHEN YOU COMIN' HOME,
TARZAN?

END OF COMPUTER CONVERSATION

I read off the message to Longh as he munched on the mango from the basket. "If the real Wallach is there, then who were we talking to . . . ?"

"I don't know," I said. "But whoever he is, he's got that copy of the satellite photos—he's probably searching for the Haunted City already. I've got to get Zan busy on this."

I switched on my portable computer and punched in the code:

COMPUTER CONVERSATION

- I NEED MORE INFO, ZAN.

- SHOOT.

- ASK PROFESSOR BRICKNOW TO PUT YOU IN TOUCH WITH MR. HENRY WALLACH. ASK WALLACH WHAT HE KNOWS ABOUT A TALL SKINNY GUY WHO WORKS FOR HIM. THE MAN IS AN EXPERT ON THE MUMMY OF THE BOY KING.

- SOUNDS LIKE A REAL FUN GUY, TARZAN.

- YEAH, YOU'D LOVE HIM. AND ANOTHER FAVOR. FIND OUT ABOUT AN OUTFIT CALLED THE ORDER OF THE PHOENIX. I'M INTERESTED IN A GUY BY THE NAME OF ORTEGA. DO YOU THINK YOU CAN HAVE ALL THAT INFORMATION FOR ME BY TOMORROW MORNING?

- HEY, NO SWEAT. JUST MAKE SURE YOU REMEMBER THIS LITTLE FAVOR.

- DON'T WORRY, ZAN. I'LL HAVE A BONUS IN YOUR PAY THIS MONTH.

- THANKS, SWEETHEART.

END OF COMPUTER CONVERSATION

Dakota King's
Microdiary Entry #5
Re: The Haunted City of Gold

It had been a hard day, and I felt exhausted. Sleep came quickly, and with it a strange dream of Longh calling to me down a dark tunnel. His voice sounded hollow and far away. I tried to ignore it, but the dream would not go away. His voice kept getting louder. Eventually I woke up, and I could still hear Longh's voice. Once my head cleared I realized it was not a dream. On the other side of the dark room I could hear Longh calling to me in a loud whisper.

"Dakota!"

"What is it?"

"I have been calling for at least an hour."

"Why didn't you just shout or come over and shake me?"

"That was not feasible. Turn on the light, but do it without getting out from your bed."

"C'mon, Longh. It's been a long day."

"Do as I ask."

The way he said that made the hair stand up on the back of my neck. Without asking any more questions, I flicked on the light. I wasn't prepared for what I saw. Crawling over Longh's face and neck were five giant, hairy tarantulas. They seemed to be in constant motion, but they never left his head.

"Longh! What happened?"

"I do not know," he said out of the side of his mouth. "All I know is about an hour ago I felt something tickling my nose. Then something tickling my neck and something else tickling the side of my face. By the streetlight outside I could see one of these things crawl up onto the bed." He did not move. One sudden move might startle the spiders into biting him.

"It doesn't make sense that they should only be on you. Why aren't they in my bed? Unless. . . ." Knowing I was safe, I jumped out of the bed and ran over to the fruit basket. I picked up a mango and sniffed it. There was the faintest smell of some kind of chemical.

That gave me an idea. I reached into my backpack and pulled out my survival knife. Then I walked over to the side of Longh's bed. The spiders didn't seem to notice me. I took the mango and cut a slice from it. Longh lay there watching me.

I cut one piece of fruit and laid it on the bed next to Longh. About twenty seconds later one of the spiders crawled over to it. The others followed a short time later. I cut another piece and laid it on the floor by the bed. The spiders climbed down and swarmed on that. I cut another and another, laying a trail of mango slices from the bed to the open window. The spiders swarmed from one piece of fruit to another and followed the trail right out the window. As soon as the last one crawled over the windowsill, I slammed the window shut.

"At first I couldn't figure out why they were only in your bed. Then I remembered—the fruit. You ate some. I didn't. I took a whiff and smelled something. It was not a typical mango smell. Since the spiders were all over your face, I guessed maybe there was some sort of chemical injected to the fruit to attract them. When you bit into the fruit, the chemical lure rubbed off on your lips. So when they smelled it, naturally they came to you.''

"Fine, but now we must determine how they came into the room.''

I walked over to the fruit basket. "I think if we take a closer look at our gift . . . aha!'' The large basket had a false bottom where the tarantulas had been hidden.

Longh picked up the fruit basket and calmly dropped it out the window. Then he went into the bathroom. To wash his face, he said.

That was a close one, Boss! I almost lost my main man.

Dakota King's
Microdiary Entry #6
Re: The Haunted City of Gold

The next morning after breakfast, I hooked up my small computer to the telephone line again and called Zan's secret number to see what she'd left on our special computer data bank. I typed in my code, and the following message came skittering across my small screen.

‼️!‼️!❗

❗❗❗❗❗❗❗

COMPUTER REPORT

● ON ITEM NUMBER ONE: WALLACH SAYS THE GUY YOU MET IS EDWARD PATCHIN, A MAN ARRESTED ONCE FOR **STEALING ARCHAEOLOGICAL TREASURES AND TRYING TO SELL THEM.** PATCHIN HAD BEEN BLACKMAILED INTO DOING IT. HE DIDN'T HAVE THE ARCHAEOLOGICAL DEGREES HE CLAIMED, AND A GROUP OF CROOKS

PRESSURED HIM INTO GRABBING SOME
TREASURE FOR THEM.

● WALLACH TOOK PITY ON THE GUY AND
RELEASED HIM IN HIS CUSTODY. HE COULD DO
THAT SINCE IT WAS PATCHIN'S FIRST OFFENSE.
WALLACH LIKES HIM BECAUSE, EVEN THOUGH
HE DOESN'T HAVE A DEGREE, HE KNOWS A LOT
ABOUT THE HAUNTED CITY OF GOLD. A HANDY
MAN FOR TREASURE HUNTERS TO KNOW.

● ON ITEM TWO: THE ORDER OF THE
PHOENIX IS A GROUP OF PEOPLE WHO THINK
THEY ARE DESCENDANTS FROM THE LANERANS
AND ARE ENTITLED TO ANY TREASURE LEFT
BEHIND BY THEM. THEIR LEADER IS ORTEGA.
HE HAS AN INTERESTING BACKGROUND. USED
TO BE A CIRCUS PERFORMER IN HIS YOUNGER
DAYS. HAD A GREAT **KNIFE-THROWING ACT,** THEY
SAY. LATER WORKED AT THE SAME UNIVERSITY
WITH PROFESSOR BRICKNOW. WAS A
CHEMISTRY TEACHER. ABOUT FOUR YEARS AGO
GOT CAUGHT UP WITH THAT PHOENIX CROWD.
HAD HIS EARLOBE TATTOOED . . . THE WHOLE
THING. BECAME A REAL CRUSADER FOR THE
CAUSE.

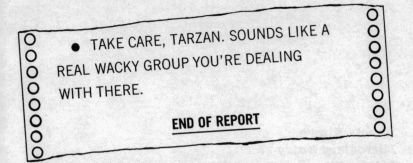

● TAKE CARE, TARZAN. SOUNDS LIKE A REAL WACKY GROUP YOU'RE DEALING WITH THERE.

END OF REPORT

As soon as the message was finished, Longh and I ambled over to the museum to talk to Patchin. When we arrived and gave our name to the guard at the door, he said Patchin had left a message for us. Over the guard's shoulder I could see a lot of official-looking people—policemen, photographers—milling around.

"Mr. Patchin says someone has stolen the medallion, and he wanted to get to the Haunted City before the thief did. He took your satellite photos with him and sends his apologies," the guard told us as if he were delivering a speech.

"He's sorry!" I shouted. "That's not going to do us any good. Can we at least go in and look at the damage?"

The guard nodded. We entered. The mummy was still in one piece, but its glass case was not. One side was smashed, and the medallion was gone. There was a small crowd of police keeping people out, but they let me and Longh pass through when we flashed one of the many fake official identification cards we always carried. Longh and I walked over to the side of the case. I noticed he was staring straight down at the floor. I followed his gaze and saw a sprinkling of dark red drops on the floor. Blood. **Whoever had broken into the case had cut his hand or arm.** I nodded to Longh that I noticed the blood, too. Then we left.

Dakota King's
Microdiary Entry #7
Re: The Haunted City of Gold

Noon found us waiting in the hot sun near the bridge on the outskirts of town. After a while Mr. Ortega showed up.

"Ah, so good of you to come, Señor. Have you your satellite photos?"

"No," I lied. "I left them back in the hotel safe. How did you known about the satellite photos?"

"There are not many secrets, even top secrets, in a small town like this. Everyone pays close attention to our visitors. But are you interested in helping us find the Haunted City?"

"Yes," I answered.

"How soon can you be packed, and ready to go, and back here?"

"About two hours," I said.

"Excellent. I think I may be of some service to you. My men and I have a good idea of the general location of the Haunted City of Gold. Once we get there, we will be able to use your photos to locate the city itself. The journey we have to make is long and complicated. At one point we will have to switch over to canoes and continue up the river."

"How long will the journey take us?" I asked.

"It will be a hard two-day trip to the river. One of

my men will be your guide. There you will meet me and some local tribesmen. Then it will take another day to paddle the rest of the way upriver to our search area. By the way, you have only the one set of satellite photos?"

"Not anymore, Mr. Ortega," I answered. "I lent one set to someone at the museum. Unfortunately, he's gone, and so are those photos."

Ortega seemed jolted by this news. "Who? Who was it?"

"We are not sure," answered Longh. "But we think it might be a Mr. Patchin."

Now Ortega appeared really shook up. "I didn't know he was out of prison!" And then, checking himself: "You are lucky to be alive. That man is an international thief, trading in my country's treasures. Some of my own people had dealings with him once, and they were lucky to escape with their lives. In these parts he is known as The Ghoul for his habit of robbing ancient graveyards."

"Whoever he is," I said, "he is also searching for the Haunted City. We must hurry to make up for lost time. C'mon, Longh, let's pack. See you in two hours, Mr. Ortega."

"We will be waiting, Señor Dakota." He reached to shake my hand, and I noticed **he had a bandage around his right hand.**

On the way back to the hotel, I could see that Longh was preoccupied. "Why is this Ortega so friendly? And why did he invent that tale about Patchin?"

"I know as much as you, Longh. Until we find out, I think we're better off keeping a good eye on him and his outfit."

I took us even less time than I thought to pack. On

the way out the hotel door, I slipped the clerk some money and asked him to take any messages that came in for us. He winked, nodded his head, and pocketed the bill. I don't know if I was getting too suspicious, but I wondered how secret any message he took for us would be. I shrugged my shoulders. What was it Ortega said? Paramar was a town with no secrets.

Longh and I got back to the bridge earlier than expected, and we found Ortega and the guide snoozing in the shade and three horses huddled together under a tree, seeking protection from the hot midday sun. As we approached, my boot scuffed a stone, and in an instant Ortega was on his feet. **In his hand was a knife.** When he saw us, he grinned and immediately put it away.

"Forgive me, Señor Dakota. There are many dangerous types around. One must be prepared for anything."

Longh and I said nothing but simply laid down our backpacks. Ortega introduced us to our guide, Miguel. When I shook his hand I noticed something distinctive about it. The **fingertip of his right index finger was missing,** just like the bearded man in the cafe! Was this yet another local society with strange symbols?

Miguel said nothing, but took our packs and started strapping them onto the pack horses. Ortega turned to us. "All right, gentlemen. Miguel will guide you to the meeting place on the riverbank. I will be going ahead—I travel faster alone—and will meet you there."

"One last question before you go, Mr. Ortega."

"Yes, of course."

"Why are you doing this for us?"

"Very simple. You are friends of Professor Bricknow. So am I. You need to go to the Haunted City of Gold. So do I. I know the ways of this jungle and its dangers. You do not. You have the photos to find it. I do not. You see the situation, Señor?'' He laughed a hearty laugh, then took one of the horses, and headed in the direction of the jungle.

The two other horses were ready, and we headed off into the bush with Miguel in the lead. The long walk into the jungle was uneventful. And quiet. Miguel said nothing as we walked. The only time he talked was to the horses when he stopped to rest them and give them some water. He kept his large hat pulled down well over his face. There wasn't much I could see of him, just a thick mustache of the type many of the peasants wore. When we stopped to rest the horses later that afternoon, I thought it might be a good opportunity to learn more about Miguel. I clicked on my microrecorder and recorded this conversation:

****

TRANSCRIPT

DK: MIGUEL.

MIGUEL: YES, SEÑOR.

DK: YOU LOOK SO FAMILIAR. HAVE I SEEN YOU ELSEWHERE? IN TOWN, PERHAPS?

MIGUEL: THAT IS NOT POSSIBLE. I HAVE ONLY JUST COME FROM MY OWN VILLAGE LAST NIGHT. I HAVE NOT BEEN TO TOWN AT ALL.

DK: I DON'T MEAN TO BE NOSY, BUT THERE IS SOMETHING VERY FAMILIAR ABOUT YOU. I HAVE THE FEELING WE HAVE MET BEFORE. AT THE RESTAURANT?

MIGUEL: OH NO, SIR. A SIMPLE PEASANT LIKE ME WOULD NOT BE COMFOR-

TABLE **SITTING OUT THERE ON THE PATIO** EATING WITH ALL THOSE FINE PEOPLE.

DK: HMMM. I GUESS I WAS MISTAKEN. SORRY TO HAVE BOTHERED YOU, MIGUEL.

MIGUEL: NO PROBLEM, SEÑOR DAKOTA.

DK: OH. ONE LAST THING, MIGUEL. DO YOU HAVE A MAP OF OUR ROUTE?

MIGUEL: YES.

DK: COULD I HAVE A LOOK AT IT?

MIGUEL: SI, HERE IT IS. [HE HANDED IT TO ME.]

DK: [I STEPPED OUT OF THE SHADE AND INTO THE BRIGHT MORNING LIGHT TO EXAMINE IT BETTER. MIGUEL WATCHED ME CAREFULLY AS I READ IT. ONE OF THE HORSES STARTED TO GET RESTLESS. HE WENT OVER TO QUIET IT. WHEN HE CAME BACK I HANDED HIM THE MAP, NEATLY FOLDED UP.] THANKS, MIGUEL. I GUESS IT'S TIME TO GET GOING.

END OF TRANSCRIPT

****

Later on the trail I found a quiet moment to talk to Longh. "Longh, keep your eye on Miguel. I have a feeling he's trouble."

"Have you any other reasons besides your 'feelings'?"

"Yes. I think he was at the outdoor restaurant when the dagger was thrown."

"Hmmm. Perhaps he is worth a little extra scrutinizing."

That evening, as Miguel prepared dinner, I signaled to Longh in sign language that we should take turns during the night watching our guide to make sure he didn't pull a fast one.

After dinner, we slipped into our sleeping bags. I was to take the first watch. But the next thing I knew it was morning and I had a splitting headache. Longh was still sleeping in the other sleeping bag.

"Longh!" I shouted. "Wake up! He's gone!" Like me, Longh had to struggle to wake up. We were both groggy and had killer headaches. Miguel must have **slipped some kind of drug into our food** and disappeared into the night.

"Now we must figure out for ourselves how to rendezvous with Ortega," Longh observed. "Unless he plans to disappear as well."

"I wouldn't worry," I said, pulling Miguel's map out of the inside of my shirt. "When I asked him for a look at this yesterday, I switched maps using my sleight-of-hand magician's skills. He never noticed how I exchanged an old road map of Indiana for his."

Longh nodded approvingly, then said, "We may have the map, Dakota, but Miguel has the horses."

I looked around. It was true. The horses were gone. "Yes, but I was smart enough to take our backpacks off the horse last night," I answered. "At least we still have those."

We also got a little lucky. As we were packing up our gear, one of the horses wandered back to camp. I called it over to me and began to unstrap one of the food sacks on its back when it whinnied and slowly sank to its knees. Not more than a few seconds later I felt something hit my chest. I looked down and saw a small feathered dart. There was one just like it in the horse's side. Fortunately, I had tucked the map inside my shirt, and that had stopped the dart.

"Longh," I yelled. "Get down! Someone's shooting poisoned darts at us." I could make out one bamboo blowpipe poking through the bushes. I signaled Longh to circle one way, while I went the other. We receded into the bushes and came up from behind. The blow-pipe was still there propped up by the bush.

Whoever had shot the darts was history—vanished. All that was left were a couple of darts and **a set of footprints.** I noticed two things: one was that **there were two nails missing from the heel of the left bootprint,** and secondly, that **the left print was sunk a little deeper into the earth than the right, indicating this person had a slight limp.** Since I never knew when I might need this information, I did an exact sketch of the print.

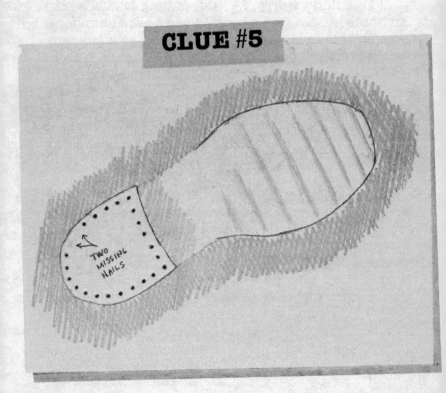

CLUE #5

TWO
MISSING
NAILS

Dakota King's
Microdiary #8
Re: <u>The Haunted City of Gold</u>

After that attack, Longh and I discussed the idea of traveling by night. While it would be harder for anyone to find us, it would take us too long to get to the rendezvous. So we would continue to travel by day, according to Longh's rules. He was the jungle expert, and everything he specified I did, no questions asked.

One of Longh's rules was never to use trails. They were the perfect place to spot anyone and to set traps. Once, without thinking, I started walking on a trail instead of hacking my own way through the bush. I had walked just a few feet when Longh waved for me to stop.

"Freeze!" he ordered.

I stood absolutely still. He pointed to a thin strand of rope stretched across the path. Carefully I stepped over it. Longh then took a long stick, hooked it on the string, and yanked hard. In seconds there was this crashing noise coming through the bushes on one side of the trail, and some giant thing came swinging across the path and smashed into a tree.

We got up and walked over for a look. Someone had made an enormous ball of mud and stuck a couple dozen sharpened bamboo spikes into it, so they were sticking out every which way. It was suspended from the trees by a long vine. If I had stumbled over the trip wire, it would have released this giant hundred-pound ball of spikes right about where my head would have been. I noticed the bamboo tips were darkened. Longh sniffed one of them. "Poisoned."

I never walked on another path after that.

After two long days hacking our way through the jungle, we came to the place on the riverbank where we were supposed to meet Mr. Ortega and his friends. As we moved toward the river, we could see smoke and hear people talking. Not knowing what to expect, we dropped our packs and slowly crawled nearer the site. We carefully peeled back the bushes and looked. Sitting around the fire were three men wearing worn-looking shirts and old beat-up hats. One of them was our friend, Mr. Ortega. I edged a little closer, and some dried leaves crunched under my weight. Mr. Ortega and his friends stopped talking and looked around them. They seemed satisfied that they had nothing to fear, and after a minute or two of silence they resumed their talking. I was just sighing a mental sigh of relief when I heard a noise behind me. "Good," I thought to myself, "he's back."

I thought it was Longh. "What do you think, Longh?" I whispered. "Does it look all right?" When I got no answer, I turned around. Longh was gone. Standing there quietly were two men, each with a blow-pipe aimed right at my head.

One of them motioned for me to stand. I did, and they had me walk ahead of them toward the fire. Hearing the noise, Mr. Ortega and his companions stood and faced in my direction. Each of them, I noticed, had the same small tattoo of the feathered bird on his earlobe. Figuring it would be worth recording—even though it might be my last, Boss—I clicked on my watch.

```
*************************************************
```

TRANSCRIPT

ORTEGA: SEÑOR DAKOTA. I DON'T BELIEVE... HOW DID YOU GET HERE?

DK: TOOK A TAXI, MR. ORTEGA. I WOULD HAVE BEEN HERE A LITTLE SOONER, BUT TRAFFIC WAS BAD.

ORTEGA: THESE... ARE MY TRUSTY GUIDES. [HE WAVED THE MEN WITH THE BLOWPIPES AWAY.] I'M SORRY IF THEY FRIGHTENED YOU. BUT HOW DID YOU MAKE IT THROUGH THAT JUNGLE? MIGUEL CAME BY A DAY OR SO AGO AND SAID SOMETHING ABOUT AN AMBUSH. WE WENT LOOKING FOR YOU BUT FOUND ONLY THE COLD REMAINS OF YOUR CAMPFIRE. WE GAVE YOU UP FOR LOST, CAPTURED BY BANDITS OR A HOSTILE TRIBE. THERE ARE PLENTY OF BOTH IN THIS AREA. AND IF THEY DIDN'T KILL YOU, THE JUNGLE WOULD. I AM IMPRESSED YOU MADE IT. I WAS GOING TO WAIT ONE MORE DAY, THEN GIVE YOU UP FOR DEAD.

DK: WHERE IS MIGUEL?

ORTEGA: I SENT HIM TO ANOTHER LAND RENDEZVOUS POINT FARTHER UPRIVER, NEAR THE HAUNTED CITY OF GOLD.

DK: SO YOU KNOW WHERE THE CITY IS?

ORTEGA: I KNOW GENERALLY WHERE IT IS. WE'LL NEED YOUR PHOTOS FOR ITS EXACT LOCATION. DO YOU HAVE THEM?

DK: [I WAS RUBBING MY EYES.] OH YES.

ORTEGA: YOU LOOK TIRED, SEÑOR DAKOTA. HERE, SIT, HAVE SOME FOOD. [I PASSED ON THAT, BOSS, HUNGRY AS I WAS. COULDN'T TRUST THE NATIVE CHOW ANYMORE.] I'LL HAVE MY MEN BRING YOUR PACK HERE AND IN THE MORNING MY PEOPLE WILL TAKE YOU UPRIVER. IT IS ONLY ONE DAY'S CANOE

RIDE. TOMORROW WE ENTER THE CITY AND BEGIN OUR HUNT FOR THE "GOLDEN WEALTH."

DK: THAT WON'T BE EASY WITHOUT THE BOY KING'S MEDALLION.

ORTEGA: ONCE WE'VE FOUND THE CITY WE'LL SEND SOMEONE BACK TO THE MUSEUM TO GET IT.

DK: I WOULDN'T TAKE ANY BETS ON THAT. THE MEDALLION WAS STOLEN A FEW DAYS AGO.

ORTEGA: [HE SEEMED GENUINELY SURPRISED.] WHO TOOK IT?

DK: WE DON'T KNOW. IT COULD HAVE BEEN ANYBODY. PATCHIN HIMSELF.

ORTEGA: NOW IT IS MORE IMPORTANT THAN EVER THAT WE... [JUST THEN SOMEONE STEPPED INTO THE EDGE OF THE CAMPFIRE LIGHT. IT WAS LONGH.]

LONGH GONH: DAKOTA. [HE NODDED TOWARD OUR HOST AND TURNED BACK TO ME.] GOOD EVENING, MR. ORTEGA. I DID NOT WANT YOU TO THINK I HAD ABANDONED YOU, DAKOTA. I DECIDED TO WAIT A LITTLE AND HEAR WHAT OUR FRIEND HAD TO SAY BEFORE I CAME OUT.

ORTEGA [OBVIOUSLY IMPRESSED BY LONGH]: YOU SEEM TO KNOW YOUR WAY AROUND A JUNGLE VERY WELL, SEÑOR GONH.

LG: THANK YOU. I SHOULD. I SPENT MOST OF MY BOYHOOD LIVING IN JUNGLES VERY MUCH LIKE YOURS. ONCE YOU LEARN TO BLEND IN WITH A WORLD LIKE THIS, THAT KNOWLEDGE NEVER LEAVES YOU.

ORTEGA: YOU, NO DOUBT, HEARD WHAT I SAID.

LG: YES, EVERY WORD. AND I AGREE. WE MUST LEAVE TOMORROW, THE EARLIER THE BETTER.

END OF TRANSCRIPT

****

Dakota King's
Microdiary Entry #9
Re: The Haunted City of Gold

The next morning we left, traveling in three dug-out canoes. Longh and I were in one, Ortega and a guide in another, and the two other guides in a third. We eased up the narrow, smooth-flowing stream, as though gliding through a green tunnel. I could tell from looking at Longh how much at ease he felt back in the jungle world he knew so well.

As a young man he had lived in Southeast Asia with some mountain tribes called the Montagnards. These people lived in the rugged jungles and low-lying mountains in that part of the world. They were as silent and deadly a group of hunters as the tigers with which they shared their jungle. While I was learning the lore and legends of the Indians in the American West, Longh was being taught the jungle survival and tracking skills of another group of people in the Far East. We had no way of knowing when we met a few years later, in a Ninja warrior training center, how similar our lives were.

As Ortega predicted, it was a long day's paddle to our landing site. When we arrived, something was not right. There was some talk up ahead. Mr. Ortega was having a long discussion with his guides. Longh, who had a natural ear for language and had already picked up a little of the local dialect, was able to translate some of the discussion.

"The guides don't want to go any farther," Longh explained. "Something about spirits or ghosts in the ancient city. I think he said even the air and water are haunted by strange beings. No one will go any farther. It appears it is just you, me, and Mr. Ortega for the rest of our journey."

Ortega came back to find us.

"I knew they would do this," Ortega said. "But I was hoping they would have stayed on with us at least a little longer. I don't know this part of the jungle very well. And if you trespass in the wrong place you can find yourself in a lot of trouble."

"What kind of trouble?" I asked.

Mr. Ortega said nothing but drew an imaginary knife across his throat. I got the point.

That night we set up camp and studied Mr. Ortega's map, comparing it with our satellite photos. From what we could tell, the city was no more than three miles inland from where we were. We all agreed we could probably be there by late the following morning.

That night as I lay sleeping, someone's hand shook me gently awake. When I finally opened my eyes, all I saw was a shadow with two bright eyes peering at me. It was Longh Gonh. He had slipped into his black Ninja costume. As silently as I could, I slipped into my own, and in a couple of minutes we had moved beyond the edge of the small camp, deep into the underbrush.

"I found the city, Dakota," Longh whispered. "Their map was inaccurate. It is only seven-eighths of a mile from here. I thought it might be productive to go ahead and have an advance look ourselves."

"Good idea, Longh. A little sneak preview never hurt."

With Longh leading the way, we moved off into the bush. In about forty minutes I could see the large hulks of some sort of buildings towering over the trees. Even in the dim starlit night they looked enormous. As we moved a few steps closer, there was an explosion of lights and noise. Blinding strobe lights kept blinking off and on, and shrieking, moaning voices—"Aaaaaa-ooooowww Aaaaaauuuuuuh"—came from the trees on our right. Then from the trees on our left. Then they were everywhere, coming out of the ground, out of the air. They were the eeriest noises I had ever heard. The hair stood up on the back of my neck. Longh and I froze.

A short time later the lights went out, and the moaning stopped. Off in the distance we heard men's voices moving slowly our way. On a signal from me, Longh and I slipped into the bushes. Eventually the men moved closer. And closer. Finally, two stopped right near the bush where I was lying on my stomach. I clicked on my recorder watch to get down what they were saying. There was some confusion, then one told the other to quiet down.

****

TRANSCRIPT

MAN 1: YOU'RE SURE IT WAS SOMEWHERE AROUND HERE?

MAN 2: THAT'S WHAT THE DETECTORS SHOWED: TWO WARM BODIES MOVING THROUGH THIS SECTION. THE EQUIPMENT DOESN'T LIE.

MAN 1: YEAH, BUT DO YOU KNOW WHAT <u>KIND</u> OF WARM BODIES THEY WERE? THEY COULD HAVE BEEN ANYTHING IN THIS BUSH—MONKEYS, CATS, LARGE BIRDS.

MAN 2: ONE OF THEM SEEMED TO MOVE LIKE A JUNGLE ANIMAL. HE WAS SPOTTED SOMEWHERE OVER THERE BY THE MOTION SENSORS. [HE POINTED OVER TOWARD WHERE LONGH WAS HIDING.] WHATEVER WE SPOTTED OVER HERE [HE POINTED IN MY DIRECTION] WAS TOO CLUMSY TO BE ANYTHING BUT A HUMAN. [CLUMSY! BOSS, DID YOU HEAR THAT?]

MAN 1: ALL RIGHT. FAN OUT. DON'T BUNCH UP. YOUR HEAT SENSORS WON'T WORK RIGHT IF YOU DO. AND YOU. . . STAY HERE. [HE TURNED A LITTLE AND BY THE GLOW OF HIS FLASHLIGHT I COULD SEE THAT **THE TIP OF THE INDEX FINGER ON HIS RIGHT HAND WAS MISSING.** HE WALKED OFF INTO THE NIGHT, LEAVING ONE OF THE MEN BEHIND.]

END OF TRANSCRIPT

****

The man standing near me held a short wand in his hand. A heat detector, I figured out. He was scanning the area around him and kept swinging it toward me. Finally he held it dead still, pointing straight at the bush where I was hiding. Longh, in the meantime, was watching from the top of a tree. At that height the heat detectors could not sense him.

The man was heading in my direction. He came to within two feet of where I was crouched. The heat detector in his had was beeping loudly. "Hey!" he shouted. "Over here! I've got something." With his other hand he pulled out his pistol.

I was trapped.

Just then Longh made some wild animal noise. The man turned, and I used the opportunity to slip out from behind the bush and stand directly behind him. I was ready for a simple Ninja trick called <u>Kasumi</u>, also known as hazing. I remained right behind him, waiting for him to turn back toward the bush.

He did, only this time I was not there. He checked his heat detector. It registered nothing. As he stood there looking confused, I began the hazing move. I reached up and snapped my fingers once just behind his right ear. He automatically looked to the right. As he turned in my direction, I raised my fingertips up to his eyes and flicked them up and down. All he saw were some white things fluttering at him out of the dark. He jerked his head back. In that instant he was totally confused.

I dropped to the ground and, as I did, I knocked the heat detector out of his hand. After he shook his head and refocused his eyes, he looked to the left and the right, but not down. I had rolled out of his field of vision, about ten feet away. I threw the heat detector as hard as I could off into the bushes. It landed with a loud crash about thirty feet behind him. He turned and ran in the direction of the noise, shouting: "Over here! Over here! They're getting away!"

After both men had run off, Longh shinnied down the tree, and he and I headed back to camp. Once we were safely back at the campsite, Longh whispered, "What do you think that was all about?"

"As near as I can figure, we set off some alarm. Whoever is there now, they're not real crazy about visitors. I can't wait until we meet them tomorrow."

Longh and I slipped back into our sleeping bags. Mr. Ortega—a sound sleeper, it seemed—never even noticed we had left the campsite and come back. I didn't bother to tape his unbroken snoring, Boss.

Dakota King's
Microdiary Entry #10
Re: The Haunted City of Gold

The next day we got up and headed the short distance down the trail to the ancient city. As we approached a break in the trees (the same place where we had been the night before), we could make out the same giant hulks. Rising through the morning mists and jungle trees was an enormous mountain of stones—a tall, narrow pyramid. On top of it was perched the main temple for this "city." As we stepped into a clearing, we saw stretched out before us a long open avenue, a stone road set into the jungle floor. At one end of the road was a large altar, near the foot of the pyramid.

On either side of the avenue was a row of stone houses, almost like miniature palaces. This line of buildings went on for at least a mile. Marking the entrance to each house was some kind of stone statue. Off in the distance, at the far end of the avenue, was a palace.

Mr. Ortega, Longh, and I stood there staring in awe at this mammoth jungle city built for no other reason than to hold the bodies of dead royalty. Animals swarmed everywhere. Birds swooped and soared over the temple, and monkeys skittered in and out of the ancient houses lined along the avenue. The heavy overgrowth of plants made the whole place look as though the vines and other plants of the jungle were trying to pull the place down stone by stone. I climbed up a few steps of the pyramid and made a sketch of what I saw.

CLUE #6

Ortega decided to investigate one of the nearby stone houses. Longh said he wanted to climb all the way to the top of the pyramid to look at the temple there. As I was sketching, I noticed off in the distance a patch of the avenue cleared out with some sort of white marking on the ground.

When I finished my drawing, I walked down for a closer look. What I found was a giant "X" on the ground made from two strips of white cloth anchored in place by large stones. Not ancient stuff, I thought. What in the name of Lanera was going on here? I began walking back toward the temple when I heard a distinct stuttering noise of an engine high in the sky. It was coming closer all the time, and while I could tell what direction it was coming from, I could not yet see it.

Seconds later there was a flash of sunlight on a windshield and I saw, rising above the treetops, a helicopter! It swooped down the ancient stone avenue making a ground-shaking racket. It headed straight for me, coming in so low it looked as if it was going to trim a few inches from my head. There was no place to hide. I threw myself to the ground.

The engine noise started to change. I looked up and saw the aircraft settle slowly down on the white "X" I had just seen. I jumped up and ran toward the helicopter. Whoever was flying that thing was going to get an earful of what I thought of his piloting skills.

By the time I reached the craft, the engine was turned off, and the blades were slowly churning down. The door opened, and out stepped the tall, skinny figure of our Mr. Patchin. As I moved toward him, I was torn between my anger about this near-miss and my curiosity about what he was doing there. Since I knew I wouldn't get much information by punching him in the nose, I decided to play it cool and listen to him. I turned on my recorder.

****

TRANSCRIPT

DK: IT'S A GOOD THING I'M NOT TALLER, I MIGHT HAVE GOTTEN A FREE HAIRCUT.

PATCHIN: MR. KING! I'M SORRY. I DIDN'T SEE YOU AT FIRST. I WAS TOO

PREOCCUPIED WITH MAKING MY LANDING. IT'S TRICKY COMING IN HERE, AND I CERTAINLY DIDN'T EXPECT ANYONE IN MY PATH. I MUST SAY I'M SURPRISED TO SEE YOU HERE. I WAS RATHER THINKING YOU WERE GOING TO WAIT UNTIL I RETURNED TO THE MUSEUM TO GET YOUR PHOTOS BACK TO YOU.

DK: WELL, I GUESS WE ARE JUST A COUPLE OF IMPATIENT TOURISTS, MR.... PATCHIN? ISN'T THAT CORRECT?

PATCHIN: AH, YES. YOU'VE DISCOVERED MY LITTLE SECRET. LET ME EXPLAIN.

DK: I'D LOVE TO HEAR IT.

PATCHIN: I AM STILL TRYING TO LIVE DOWN A PERSONAL, UH, MISCALCULATION AND WAS RELUCTANT TO TELL ANYONE WHO I WAS UNTIL THE SCANDAL OF WHAT I DID PASSED. AS YOU NO DOUBT HAVE LEARNED, I DID ONCE GET INVOLVED WITH AN UNSAVORY GROUP OF PEOPLE. BUT MR. WALLACH WAS KIND ENOUGH TO GIVE ME A JOB. NOT JUST OUT OF CHARITY. I AM AN EXPERT IN MANY ARCHAEOLOGICAL MATTERS. RATHER THAN LET THAT EXPERIENCE GO TO WASTE, MR. WALLACH HIRED ME TO HELP HIM AT THE MUSEUM.

DK: I UNDERSTAND THAT. BUT WHY DID YOU LET US BELIEVE YOU WERE WALLACH?

PATCHIN: I SAW NO HARM IN IT. LOOK, MR. KING. I AM TRYING TO LIVE DOWN A BAD REPUTATION. I DIDN'T KNOW HOW YOU WOULD REACT ONCE YOU WERE TOLD WHO I REALLY WAS. OF COURSE, ONCE THE MEDALLION WAS GONE IT BECAME EVEN MORE AWKWARD.

DK: YES. AND I THINK IT'S RATHER INTERESTING HOW YOU JUST HAPPENED TO TURN UP HERE SHORTLY AFTERWARDS.

PATCHIN: MY FRIENDS [HE POINTED TO A MAN AND A WOMAN APPROACHING] ARE WHY I'M HERE. THEY HAD ALREADY FIGURED OUT THE APPROXIMATE LOCATION OF THE HAUNTED CITY, BUT YOUR SATELLITE PHOTOS GREATLY SIMPLIFIED THEIR SEARCH.

I'VE BEEN WORKING WITH SOME OF MY CRONIES WHO HAVE ALSO GONE STRAIGHT. I PERSUADED MR. WALLACH TO HIRE THEM TO HELP ME SEARCH FOR THE CITY. THEY KNOW THIS JUNGLE PRETTY WELL. BY THE SCRAPS OF EVIDENCE THEY FOUND—STONE CARVINGS SCATTERED THROUGH THE BUSH, STORIES BY LOCAL TRIBESMEN ABOUT GIANT MOUNTAINS MADE BY MEN—THEY KNEW THEY WERE GETTING CLOSER. BUT THE JUNGLE HERE IS SO THICK, THE EMPIRE STATE BUILDING COULD BE IN HERE, AND YOU MIGHT WALK BY IT. YOUR PHOTOS WERE JUST THE TICKET. IN A FEW DAYS WE WERE ABLE TO ZERO IN ON THE PLACE AND GET WHAT WE NEEDED. AH, MY FRIENDS. [THE MAN AND WOMAN WALKED UP TO US.]

MR. DAKOTA KING, I'D LIKE YOU TO MEET MY COLLEAGUES: ALLEGRA MCGORY, MY ASSISTANT AND COPILOT, AND ALPHONSE—BETTER KNOWN AS AL—DANK, MY RIGHT-HAND MAN. [EVEN BEFORE I SAW DANK'S **INDEX FINGER WITH THE TIP MISSING**, I KNEW WHO THIS NOW CLEAN-SHAVEN GUY WAS—NONE OTHER THAN THE GUY I HAD SEEN IN THE CAFE AND OUR SO-CALLED GUIDE, MIGUEL. MINUS HIS BEARD AND MUSTACHE, DANK LOOKED LIKE A YANKEE. WHAT KIND OF "COLLEAGUE" HE WAS WASN'T YET CLEAR.]

DK: NICE TO SEE YOU AGAIN, MIGUEL, OR IS DANK YOUR CURRENT NAME?

PATCHIN: VERY GOOD, MR. KING. YOUR POWERS OF OBSERVATION ARE QUITE REMARKABLE. [AL SAID NOTHING, BUT STARED HARD AT ME WITH HIS BEADY LITTLE EYES. I COULDN'T TELL FROM HIS EXPRESSION IF HE WANTED TO

MAKE SOME COMMENT OR PULL OUT THE PISTOL IN HIS HOLSTER AND SHOOT A HOLE IN ME.] UPON PROFESSOR WALLACH'S INSTRUCTIONS, I HAD AL KEEP AN EYE ON YOU DURING YOUR VISIT. WHEN MR. ORTEGA WAS LOOKING FOR A JUNGLE GUIDE, I ARRANGED FOR MR. DANK HERE TO INTERVIEW FOR THE JOB.

WELL, LET'S CONTINUE WITH OUR LITTLE TOUR. THE "CITY," AS YOU SEE, IS ONE LONG STREET. DOWN THERE [HE POINTED IN THE DIRECTION FROM WHICH I CAME] IS THE TEMPLE WHERE THE LANERAN PRIESTS PERFORMED THEIR CEREMONIES. AND THERE [HE POINTED TO THE OTHER END OF THE AVENUE] IS THE PALACE WHERE THE REIGNING RULER OF THE HAUNTED CITY RESIDED. AS EACH KING OR QUEEN DIED, THEIR BODIES WERE MOVED INTO THE BIG PALACE. WHOEVER WAS THERE BEFORE WAS MOVED OUT INTO ONE OF THESE SMALLER "PALACES" ON THE SIDE OF THE STREET THAT WAS BUILT FOR THEM. AS THE LEGENDS SAY, THE LAST RULER TO OCCUPY THAT PALACE WAS THE FATHER OF THE DEAD BOY KING. FOR REASONS I TOLD YOU ABOUT THE OTHER DAY, THEY BURIED THE BOY ELSEWHERE. WE KNEW WHERE THAT WAS, AND WE NOW KNOW THIS IS THE TRUE HAUNTED CITY OF GOLD.

DK: SO WHERE IS THIS GOLD ANYWAY?

PATCHIN: IT'S HARD TO SAY. IT COULD BE ANYWHERE HERE. UNTIL WE ARE ABLE TO GET OUR HANDS ON THE GOLD MEDALLION, WE WILL ONLY BE ABLE TO GUESS. BUT AT LEAST WE KNOW WHERE TO START—AH, HELLO, MR. GONH.

END OF TRANSCRIPT

****

Dakota King's
Microdiary Entry #11
Re: The Haunted City of Gold

Just then Longh approached. "Dakota, I want you to come to the top of that pyramid sometime today. There's a . . . ." He stopped talking when he saw Patchin and the others standing next to me. "Mr. Wallach. We meet again."

"It's okay, Longh. He knows that we know he's Patchin. And so now we all know. These are his associates. Ms. McGory, his copilot. And, of course, you already know Miguel, but now he would like to be called Al Dank."

"Yes, of course," Longh replied, without a blink.

Seeing the group, Ortega walked over to investigate. His eyes shifted from one face to another before settling on Patchin.

"Hello, Patchin," he said coolly.

"Morning, Ortega. Enjoying your visit to my little city?" he asked tauntingly.

Ortega ignored this and turned to Longh and me. "I'm going to set up camp near the base of the temple. You can bring your equipment there later, if you wish." Then he walked away without waiting for an answer.

Longh had brought over both our backpacks, and we each stood there with them slung over one shoulder.

"You are invited to join us, if you prefer," said Patchin. "Our camp is at the other end of the avenue, by the large palace. But of course it's up to you." His colleagues standing around him said nothing, but simply glared at us.

"We appreciate the offer, Patchin," I said. "But we've been traveling together so long I think we'll keep it that way."

Patchin said nothing but nodded in agreement. He and his friends withdrew, heading back down the other end of the avenue.

As they were leaving, I turned to Longh and asked what it was he had to tell me.

"There is an odd structure on top of the temple pyramid I think you had better look at. I have some ideas about it and want to see if you agree."

"Sure, Longh, but first I want to make a sketch of the layout of this area." I pulled out my sketchpad and pencil. I dropped the pencil, and as I reached down I noticed a footprint in the dirt. There was something about the footprint that bothered me. And then it hit me all at once: **it had the same left heel—with two missing nails—as the footprint we found near the ambush point where someone shot poisoned darts at us. Only the distinctive limp mark was missing.**

"Quick," I asked Longh urgently, "who was standing here just before?"

"You, me, Ortega, Patchin, and his associates. Why?"

"Because I think whoever has been trying to make life difficult for us is among them."

"Hmmm," mused Longh, looking at the footprint. "I suppose I could safely assume our troubles are not over yet."

"That's putting it mildly. We've got a real bad

bunch of boys here. One of them is a thief, and someone has been trying hard to be a murderer as well.''

''Who do you think it is?'' asked Longh.

''Darned if I know,'' I answered. ''I've got some other things to worry about now. Let's go to the top of this pyramid. You can show me what you've found, and I'll make my sketches from up there.''

It was a long, hard climb to the top. There must have been two million steps there. No wonder the Lanerans only held their ceremonies a few times each year. Once I got up there and was able to breathe again, I did a quick sketch outlining the whole area.

"Now, Longh," I asked when I had finished my drawing. "What was it you wanted to show me?"

"This," he said, leading me over to one side of the doorway of the temple. Drilled through the thick stone wall was a large hole that looked like a miniature tube. On the inside of the wall, just under the hole, was a small ledge. On the outside of the wall, the hole was plugged up with something, but there was a small hole, a little smaller than a keyhole, drilled through that plug.

"If you look down this tube-shaped hole," Longh said, "you will see that it is pointed down toward the avenue below us."

I took a look for myself. It was like peering down a small tunnel. Through the small hole at the other end I could see a lot of the stone avenue.

"Very interesting, Longh. But so what?"

"Just a theory, mind you, but I think this tube hole is the key to locating the 'golden wealth,'" he said in a hush.

"And I think you have found one hole in a wall and maybe another in your head. Why do you figure this has anything to do with the treasurer?"

"My theory, Dakota, is based on three things. First, it is a generally known fact that the important center of life in these ancient jungle cultures was the temple. So, I ask you, why should it be any different with the Lanerans? For that reason I decided to climb the temple first and have a look around up here."

"Where you found a hole," I said, still unimpressed.

"Second," Longh continued, ignoring my comment, "I knew that where a temple is built, and the direction it faces, is also very important. So I paid particular attention to the direction this temple faced and looked carefully at the area around the front of the tube hole where"—he beckoned me outside with his crooked finger—"I found this." He pulled away some vines and jungle growth to reveal a carving on the plugged-up side of the hole.

CLUE #7

"It's the bird again! The one from the medallion and Ortega's ear!" I said in surprise.

"Very good, Dakota. And do you notice anything else?"

"It has a hole in it, too."

"Yes. This is what is blocking up the peephole you

were just looking through. Which brings me to point number three: the theory. You remember that the medallion is supposed to be the guide to the treasure?"

"Yeah . . . well, that was the legend. All we know is that it somehow was supposed to help find the 'golden wealth' of the Lanerans."

Longh nodded his head and led me back inside the temple. "Now I will bet that when you put the medallion in this cut in the rock," he said, pointing to the ledge, "you get a crude but efficient sight. So when the hole in the medallion, here, is aligned with the hole in the stone carving of the bird, at the other end of the tube, what you see when you peer through the hole is . . ."

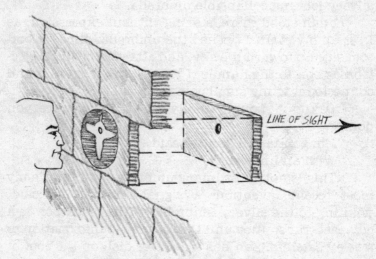

LINE OF SIGHT

". . . where the treasure is buried!" I finished the sentence for him. "That's brilliant, Longh. But there's one problem. Now that the medallion has been stolen, we'll never know if your idea is any good. Which brings me to point four," I said. "We have to devise a way to flush out the guy who has it."

"How do you know that he is here? Or, if he is, that he has it with him, Dakota?"

"I don't. But I'm willing to bet that if he is here, he's got the medallion with him or has hidden it so he can get to it fast. We have to figure out a way to make him <u>want</u> to take it out. In fact, while we're up here I think I'll make a call."

And without saying anything more, I scrambled down the face of the pyramid as fast as I could go. I grabbed my backpack, which I had left down at the bottom and, minutes later, I struggled back up with it on my back. I dug out my compact computer, little more than a keyboard with a small screen, a little electronic box about the size of two packs of cigarettes, and a silvery-looking collapsible umbrella.

Longh stood there, staring without expression, as I set up my stuff. I opened the umbrella, aimed it bottom side up toward the sky, and attached my little electronics box to the handle. I took a wire from that and connected it to my small computer.

"Dakota," Longh finally asked. "What are you doing?"

"I'm gonna call Zan," I said.

"With an umbrella?"

"This is not an ordinary umbrella, Longh; it's my most recent invention—a signal reflector," I said, pointing to the silvery umbrella. "This black box is a compact transmitter unit that beams up information to a relay satellite. Zan has a receiver dish on the roof of her computer building to receive what I send."

Longh just stared, fascinated by the setup and envisioning how useful this compact item would be to us in the future. I picked up my keyboard and typed in the code. Once I got a go-ahead signal, I began typing my message:

COMPUTER CONVERSATION

TO: ZAN

FROM: TARZAN

RE: THE HAUNTED CITY OF GOLD

I NEED YOUR HELP ON THIS ONE, ZAN. PLEASE SEND A MESSAGE TO MY HOTEL WARNING ME OF A VOLCANIC ERUPTION SOON IN THE AREA OF THE HAUNTED CITY.

END OF COMPUTER CONVERSATION

About twenty minutes went by before my computer started beeping at me. I had an incoming message:

"Okay, we're all set," I said to Longh as I gathered up my equipment. "The trap is set. Now we watch and wait. Let's go wash up and relax a little. This could take awhile."

Looking a little mystified, but knowing better than to start asking a lot of questions, Longh helped me pack up. We climbed down the pyramid and there, waiting at the bottom, was Patchin. He invited us to share dinner with him and his crew that night.

"Is Mr. Ortega invited?" I asked.

"Yes, but he declined to come."

It was no surprise Ortega had turned them down, considering what he thought of Patchin. But I figured this might be an opportunity to learn a little more about what Patchin and his gang were doing there. Longh and I had no intention of eating their food, of course, so we chowed down ahead of time. Longh had a healthy bowl of vegetable mush, and I ate my last candy bar.

Dakota King's
Microdiary Entry #12
Re: The Haunted City of Gold

We headed back to our campsite to wash up. Ortega was there, sitting quietly by a small campfire preparing his dinner. He looked up as we approached.

"You agreed to eat with that crook?"

"Who knows, it might prove interesting," I said. "Why aren't you coming, Ortega?" I asked. "There might be safety in numbers."

"I don't trust him," he said, "and I don't think you should either. He and his band of crooks are after something from you. My advice is to stay away. I have bad enough feelings about this place as it is. And he is nothing but trouble. I feel it."

I still said I disagreed. Ortega simply shrugged his shoulders and went back to tending the fire. Longh came by and said we were short on water. He was going to fill the canteens from the pool near Patchin's campsite.

"Stay away from those waters!" Ortega said so suddenly it startled me and Longh. "Legends say that both the air and water are haunted by the spirits of the dead. They should not be disturbed." He stared at us with a wild-eyed look.

"I do not think the spirits would mind lending us a couple of canteens of water," Longh said with a gentle smile. As with most unsuperstitious people, the superstitions of others amused him. "I promise to pour back what I do not use."

"Don't make jokes," Ortega said, almost shouting. "There is truth to those legends."

Longh shook his head, picked up the canteens, and walked off into the bush. Our special water purifying pills usually took care of any problems with strange drinking water. I prepared my bedding and mosquito netting for later, then took out my drawing of the city to study it. If Longh's theory was right, the golden treasure was somewhere out there within view of the temple. But it was a huge place, I thought. It could take years to find it.

I was folding up the drawing when I heard a bloodcurdling scream. At first I thought it was an animal in pain, but the second time I realized it was a human voice. And when I realized it was Longh's voice, my heart stopped. In seconds I found myself running hard through the jungle in the direction of the noise.

It was coming from the pool.

When I got there Longh was lying on his back, stiff as a board. His eyes were locked wide open, staring straight up at the sky. Clutched in one hand was a canteen with water still glugging out of it. At first I thought he was dead. Then he screamed again in that horrifying, unearthly scream I had just heard. It went through me like an icy wind. Never, through our worst ordeals, had I ever heard Longh's voice raised. Never.

I grabbed him by the shoulders and shouted his name. He continued screaming.

"Dakota! My legs! My legs!"

"What's the matter with your legs?" He stared straight past me.

"They are two giant snakes. Do you not see them?

They have curled up on their tails and are trying to swallow me. I can smell their poisonous breath on my face. Get away, Dakota. Save yourself.''

There was nothing wrong with his legs or with any other part of his body that I could see. I looked at the canteen. I looked at Longh. There was water trickling out of the side of his mouth. Maybe Ortega was right. The waters were cursed.

I heard footsteps. Patchin and Dank had heard the screaming and came running from their campsite.

''What happened?'' Patchin wanted to know.

''I don't know,'' I said. ''He's seeing things. He's convinced his legs have turned into snakes or something.''

Dank look at Longh lying there, noticed the canteen, and asked, ''Did he drink any of this water?'' He pointed to the pool.

''I don't know,'' I answered. ''He may have.''

Patchin quickly looked around, ran over to a bush, and yanked some leaves off a branch. ''Give him these. Tell him to chew on them. Make him chew them.''

''Only if you eat some first,'' I said immediately. Patchin might have been trying to help, but he might also have been trying to bump one of us off for good.

''Very well, Mr King,'' he said, stuffing a wad of the leaves into his mouth.

I watched to make sure he didn't palm the leaves, then I grabbed some. ''Longh, listen to me.'' Longh was lying there, wild-eyed. ''Longh,'' I said. ''Eat this. It will get rid of the snakes.''

I managed to stuff some leaves into his mouth. ''Now, chew.'' Automatically he began chewing. I gave him a couple more leaves. After a minute or two he seemed calmer. A little while later he spit out a wad of leaves, closed his eyes, and went to sleep.

"Sorry I doubted you. What are these, anyway?" I asked Patchin.

He said the leaves would counteract the poisons that had given Longh his crazy visions. He pointed to some jungle plants growing by the edge of the water and said that whenever they came into bloom their buds released a natural poison into the water. In time, the water was saturated with a tasteless chemical that affected the brain of anyone unlucky enough to drink it. Some jungle tribes, he said, used the sap from these plants to tip their poison darts.

Fortunately for Longh, Patchin had studied the plants and knew that the cure for the poison was another plant that grew nearby.

"What I don't understand," he said, "is why this poison pool wasn't marked. Usually these ancient peoples left a warning marker of a carved figure of some sort of demon. We found one near another pool just the other day."

As he was telling me this, I scanned the shoreline. Not far from where Longh had fallen was a low flat block of stone, dark from centuries of being weather-worn. But there was one light patch on it, as though something had just been taken from there recently. As I stepped closer to where the stone was, I noticed an odd-shaped object lying in the water reeds. Wading out into the water I reached down and lifted it out. I had in my hand one of the strangest carved figures I had ever seen: a bald, toothless fiend with empty eye sockets and fingers that looked like bolts of electricity. To get a record of this strange thing, I later did a sketch of it for Dr. Bricknow's archaeological files.

"Is this one of those figures?" I held it up to Patchin.

"Yes, that's exactly it."

"It looks like someone took him off his pedestal and threw him in the water recently—the reeds in the water look newly bent." I said. "Maybe as a joke."

"If it's a joke, it's a dangerous one," said Patchin. "These are powerful drugs. Your friend is lucky to be alive."

Longh started to come to. We told him what happened while he was out. He sat there, listening attentively, then thanked Patchin for saving his life. Patchin and Dank headed back to their camp. Unfortunately, they were both wearing sandals, so my quick check of their prints yielded nothing useful. We agreed to meet later, as planned, for dinner.

Longh struggled to his feet, still a little unsteady from his experience. I told him what Patchin had said. He took it all in, and after a minute or two of silence said: "You know, Dakota, there are two things that are obvious from what happened. Whoever threw away that figure was deliberately trying to get either you or me or Ortega. Secondly, **whoever ditched that figure had to be some kind of expert about the Laneran society to know what that figure meant.**"

Dakota King's
Microdiary Entry #13
Re: The Haunted City of Gold

When we got back to our camp, we told Ortega about what had happened at the pool. We described the events as they happened and explained the strange effects of the poisons Longh had gotten into his system. He listened without much sympathy (which didn't surprise us too much), and all he could manage to say was: "I told you so."

Later that evening, cleaned up and refreshed, we ambled over to Patchin's campsite. I got my recorder watch ready. They were waiting for us and seemed concerned about Longh's health. When he assured them he was in good shape, we settled down and had dinner. That is, the others had dinner, while Longh and I went through the motions of eating without actually doing so. I'd volunteered to clean up, so no one noticed that Longh and I hadn't touched our food.

Later, when we were a little more relaxed, we sat down and began to talk. Patchin and Ms. McGrory, his copilot, were summoned away. There was a radio in Patchin's tent, and there was a message coming through for him. That left me and Longh with Dank. I decided to take the chance and check out a hunch I had about Dank. I clicked on my recorder.

****

TRANSCRIPT

DK: MR. DANK, THAT IS AN EXCELLENT PAIR OF BOOTS YOU HAVE THERE. WOULD YOU MIND IF I TOOK A CLOSER LOOK?

DANK: NOPE. GO AHEAD.

DK: I'M PARTICULARLY INTERESTED IN THE WAY YOUR SOLES ARE DESIGNED. I'M ALWAYS LOOKING FOR GOOD BOOTS. EVERYTHING IS SO SLIPPERY IN THE JUNGLE. [BOSS, I GUESS YOU KNOW WHY I WAS LOOKING AT THE SOLE OF HIS BOOTS. **I WANTED TO SEE IF THERE WERE TWO NAILS MISSING FROM ONE OF THE HEELS. BUT THERE WEREN'T.**] THANKS. I'LL HAVE TO KEEP MY EYE OUT FOR A PAIR LIKE THIS. TELL ME, MR. DANK. WHY HAVE YOU BEEN SO MYSTERIOUS—THAT LITTLE SPYING JOB IN THE CAFE, POSING AS A GUIDE...

DANK: I'M SORRY, MR. KING, I CAN'T TELL YOU. [WITHOUT SAYING A WORD, I ROLLED BACK MY SLEEVE, LETTING HIM SEE THE SMALL TATTOO OF THE EAGLE PUT THERE YEARS AGO BY THE INDIAN TRIBE I HAD STAYED WITH AS A BOY. AMONG CERTAIN SECRET ORGANIZATIONS OF THE WORLD I AM KNOWN BY MY CODE NAME, EAGLE, AND THE FACT THAT I HAVE A TATTOO OF ONE. THOSE WHO KNOW THE NAME ALSO KNOW OF THE TATTOO. I COULD TELL DANK IMMEDIATELY RECOGNIZED IT. HE LEANED OVER FOR A CLOSER LOOK.] MR. KING, VERY INTERESTING TATTOO YOU HAVE THERE. [HE PAUSED BEFORE CONTINUING TALKING.] I SUPPOSE IT IS SAFE TO TELL YOU. I'M AN UNDERCOVER AGENT HIRED BY MY GOVERNMENT TO KEEP AN EYE ON THIS WHOLE OPERATION. I WORKED WITH PATCHIN ONCE BEFORE AS AN UNDERCOVER AGENT, ONLY BACK THEN HE THOUGHT I WAS REALLY A SMUGGLER. NOW HE THINKS I'M A REFORMED SMUGGLER. HE NEVER REALLY LEARNED MY TRUE IDENTITY.

My government wants to protect this place from looters. I asked for this assignment, but I'll tell you, there are safer jobs to have. The people who loot and steal from these archaeological sites don't play by any rules. I had the tip of one finger shot off by one gang of them. As you have learned by now there are certain people who prefer that you or anyone who is an official not come here at all.

DK: Like who?

DANK: Like whoever it was who shot that poisoned dart at you or threw away the warning figure at the poisoned waterhole.

DK: Why should I trust you?

LONGH GONH: Yes. For example, why did you desert us when you were pretending to be our guide?

DANK: I didn't desert you. I woke up early because something spooked the pack horses. They got away. By the time I got back to your camp, you two were gone, and there was one very groggy horse standing around. I tried to pick up your trail, but I lost you in the brush.

DK: Why weren't you drugged by the food?

DANK: In my work I've learned to be careful. I had brought my own food and ate that. Don't forget you ate what had been loaded on the horses.

DK: Why all those ghost sounds and those lights?

DANK: Just trying to scare as many people as possible from snooping around here. I rigged up some simple electronic sensors all around this place. No one gets in or out without setting off the

ALARMS. TO MAYBE SCARE OFF SOME JUNGLE TRIBESMEN OR THE ODD JUNGLE WANDERER, WE ALSO PLAY LOUD TAPES FROM HORROR MOVIES. YOU KNOW, SHRIEKS AND SCREAMS. THAT KIND OF THING. IT USUALLY DOES THE TRICK. THE LEGENDS ABOUT GHOSTS AND SUCH HELPS. [HE LOOKED AT US AND SMILED.] SO. THAT WAS YOU GUYS LAST NIGHT! WELL, I'M NOT SURPRISED.

RIGHT NOW I HAVE BIGGER PROBLEMS. I'VE GOT TO FIND WHO TOOK THE MEDALLION. MY GOVERNMENT WILL WANT TO START EXCAVATING HERE, AND I KNOW MY CHIEF WILL WANT TO KNOW WHERE WE CAN FIND THE GOLDEN TREASURE. AND AS YOU KNOW, WITHOUT THAT MEDALLION, IT COULD TAKE A LOT OF DIGGING BEFORE WE GET LUCKY.

END OF TRANSCRIPT

****

The conversation was cut short when we all heard a sharp crack, the sound of someone stepping on a stick, and some scrambling in the bushes. Instantly we were all on our feet and running in the direction of the noise.

Longh and I were going flat out, but something or someone else was moving really fast. We couldn't seem to gain on him. Then the sound of running stopped and was followed by a racket directly overhead. Longh stopped, listened, and got a fix on the noise. He aimed his flashlight...up. Shining back at us like two car reflectors were the eyes of a wild-eyed monkey.

Annoyed with this false alarm, we headed back to the campfire. When we were about fifteen feet away from it, Longh dropped to his knees and studied the ground. Dank and I both followed his flashlight beam with our eyes. The beam stopped at a broken branch. Near it was another. All around was some flattened grass. Following a trail only he seemed to see, Longh walked farther into the bush until all we could see was the distant glow from his flashlight. A minute or two later, I heard him call out.

"Over here!"

I made my way through the bush and Longh stood there shining his light straight at the ground. Pressed into the moist jungle earth was **the imprint of a boot heel with two nails missing. Whoever it was had what was getting to be a familiar limp.**

"Is that our man?" I asked Longh. He said nothing, but nodded his head.

"How long has that print been there?" I asked. He picked up some of the dirt, pinched it between his fingers, and let it slowly trickle out. "Fifteen, twenty minutes. Whoever was here probably overheard all that we said. When we ran out after the monkey, our spy probably just kept still and waited until we passed right by him, before he scooted off himself."

"Which way did he go?" I asked.

"Toward the avenue," Longh said. "But it is not worth following. Once he gets out on that stone pavement his trail will be impossible to pick up without a bloodhound."

We turned and walked slowly back to the campfire. When we got there Patchin was waiting, **looking a little out of breath and sweaty,** I noticed. He seemed relieved and a little surprised to see us. He still had on his sandals, so I couldn't check out that boot theory of mine.

We told him the story of the noise and the monkey. He, in turn, had something equally interesting for us. **"I was just on the radio, and I've been told by someone back at Paramar that seismologists think there's going**

**to be a big earthquake in this area very soon, in the
next couple of weeks.** If that happens we'll never find
the treasure, and priceless archaeological items will be
destroyed. I want to get started on searching this place
tomorrow.

"Dank," he said, turning to the man, "have Allegra
get the chopper ready. We're going to need to fly in some
more supplies. I want to take off by tomorrow
morning."

He turned back to all of us. "I guess I'll call it a
night. It looks like we all have a big day ahead of us
tomorrow."

On the way back to our own campsite, Longh and I
discussed what happened that night. "It's kind of
interesting, don't you think," I asked Longh, "that
Patchin just happened to be away when that spy in the
bushes was there?"

"And equally curious," added Longh, "that he
was aware of the fake earthquake warning. Still, it
could be just a coincidence he was gone all that time.
And maybe we will have a real earthquake."

With that cheery thought bouncing around in our
heads, we walked the rest of the way to camp in silence.
When we got there, Ortega was already in his sleeping
bag and snoring, his boots wedged underneath the bag.
I realized I had never checked the bottom of his boots.
Carefully I eased his left boot out from underneath
him, turned it over, and quickly shone the flashlight
on the heel. But I couldn't see anything. There was too
much mud on it. There was no way of knowing whether
they even had nails, let alone two tiny missing nails.
Ortega groaned a bit and stirred as though he were
about to wake up. Quickly I slid the boots back under
him.

Dakota King's
Microdiary Entry #14
Re: The Haunted City of Gold

    The next day passed uneventfully. Almost. While Longh and I explored the large Palace of the Dead at the end of the avenue, I happened to glance out of one of the narrow stone peepholes in the side of the building facing the temple. There was a flash of light from the top of the temple, like the sun bouncing off a mirror. I told Longh to look. He saw it, too.

    "What do you think, Longh?"

    "It could be many things, but it you will allow me to speculate, I think it is our mysterious thief and that flash is the medallion he is fitting into that peephole."

    "Let's go!"

    We bolted out the door and down the dozens of palace steps to the ground, running as fast as we could. We slipped to the side of the avenue to stay a little out of sight, hoping whoever it was hadn't seen us yet. Out of breath and sweating, we reached the bottom of the pyramid at the same time. I gave a signal to Longh. He ran up the back. I ran up the front, slipping on the broken and wobbly steps all the way. But by the time we reached the top, whoever was there had gone. We did find tracks in the fine dirt around the doorway. (Longh had brushed over the area with a branch from a nearby bush the day before.) There they were: the same

limp and the boot tracks with two nails missing.

"What is this?" Longh asked, poking through some other bushes. "Our visitor carelessly dropped something." And he held up in his hand **a small double-edged dagger, the kind that almost redesigned my face our first day in Paramar.** Further searching turned up nothing more.

I decided maybe it was time to find out a little more about our friend Miguel, or Dank, or whoever he was. I went down and got my communications equipment. Back up at the temple, I sent a message off to Zan asking her to track down any and every foreign secret agent working on the Haunted City of Gold. I doubted Miguel's name was Miguel or even Dank, so I gave her a description of him. I told her to leave a message for me that night on satellite hookup.

When we got back to camp we found a barefoot Ortega sitting by a fire. I scanned the ground for the telltale bootprints. No luck—just our own footprints and Ortega's barefoot ones. As I asked him if he had seen anyone running this way, I tried to get a glimpse into his open pack. (He had always been very secretive about what he had in there. Irreplaceable maps, he told me.) Ortega said he had seen no one. Carrying his boots, he said he was going to fill his canteen—hopefully from a non-haunted stream.

While he was gone I took a quick look inside his backpack. Sure enough, there were some copies of ancient maps from the days of the Spanish explorers. And a few other interesting things: like **a small two-way radio and a block of what looked like white clay with some wires sticking out of it. Tucked way in the back was a flight schedule for a U.S. airline.** Ortega came back abruptly, so I quickly turned and acted fascinated with my bootlaces.

And as I knelt there tying my bootlace, all I could think was: We missed him again. But this, I promised myself, was the last time. We had to force this guy into the open.

That evening I snuck back up to the temple, where I had hidden my gear, and got my hookup with Zan:

!.!!*!*!*!

COMPUTER REPORT

HEY JUNGLE BOY!

I RAN A CHECK ON ALL GOVERNMENT AGENTS INVOLVED IN THE LANERA OPERATION. I TURNED UP TWO LIKELY CANDIDATES: ARTURO CERVANTES AND HIS BROTHER HECTOR. I THINK YOU CAN RULE OUT HECTOR, BECAUSE HE DISAPPEARED MYSTERIOUSLY A FEW YEARS AGO CHASING DOWN SOME ARCHAEOLOGICAL ROBBERS. RUMOR IS THEY HELPED HIM "DISAPPEAR."

THAT LEAVES HIS BROTHER ARTURO, ONE OF THE TOP AGENTS AND A **MASTER OF DISGUISE.** EVER SINCE THIS BROTHER DROPPED OUT OF SIGHT HE HAS BEEN SPENDING HIS TIME TRYING TO CATCH ANY AND ALL ROBBERS HE CAN FIND. THAT'S HOW

HE ENDED UP WORKING WITH PATCHIN IN THE
HOPES OF MEETING OTHER ROBBERS. HE
DIDN'T KNOW PATCHIN WAS A ONE-TIME
CROOK. RUMOR IS THAT OL' ARTURO HAS
BEEN SPENDING TOO MUCH TIME IN THE
JUNGLE AND IS A LITTLE LOOPY. AT ANY RATE,
THIS ARTURO CHARACTER SOUNDS LIKE ONE
TOUGH CUSTOMER IF YOU GET ON THE
WRONG SIDE OF HIM. HE'S A BIT OF A REBEL
AGENT, SO WATCH OUT. SOME OF THESE
INTELLIGENCE GUYS GET A LITTLE WEIRD AND
A LITTLE TOO INDEPENDENT WHEN THEY'RE
OUT IN THE BUSH TOO LONG WITHOUT A BOSS
TO KEEP THEM IN LINE.

SO YOU BE A GOOD BOY NOW, HEAR?

END OF REPORT

Dakota King's
Microdiary Entry #15
Re: The Haunted City of Gold

The next day we announced to Patchin, Dank, and Ortega that now that the city had been found, the important part of our mission was over. We planned to return home. After us would come a team of specialists to try and locate the treasure. We made a big deal of getting the canoes ready and paddling out on the river.

Two hours later, we quietly eased over to the riverbank farther downriver, shouldered our backpacks, and headed back to the Haunted City of Gold.

We tried to get there just before nightfall, but the jungle was so dense we arrived after dark had fallen. Finding a secluded spot, we changed into our Ninja clothing to make us less visible in the dark. Then we moved in on the city.

There was noise and loud talking near Patchin's camp, so we slunk over that way. When we got close enough to see, we were more than mildly surprised by what we saw. Patchin, Dank, and Ortega were sitting down together. Apparently they didn't hate each other anymore. They were toasting each other with glasses of wine that **Ortega poured from a bottle.** He didn't seem to be drinking as much as the others. We watched for a while longer, but since nothing much seemed to be happening we slipped back into the night. We settled down at our camp and conked out right away. We were exhausted from a hard day's paddling and hiking. I woke up once in the middle of the night. I thought I heard thunder, but I looked up and the sky was cloudless. I shrugged my shoulders and went back to sleep.

The first thing that awoke us the next morning was the sound of a helicopter, Patchin's helicopter, roaring overhead. We got out of our sleeping bags in a flash, yanked on our clothes and boots, and ran as fast as we could toward the Haunted City. I headed toward Patchin's camp, while Longh went to have a look at Ortega's camp. I carefully stole up to Patchin's area. Empty. The camping equipment—the tents, the stove, the lanterns—was still set up, but not a soul was in sight. The bottle of wine from the previous night was still sitting on the table. Automatically I sniffed the bottle. Something more than wine had been in there.

A short while later Longh came running back from Ortega's campsite.

"Anything?" I asked.

Longh shook his head. "No trace of him or any of his camping equipment. He has disappeared. Have you had any luck?"

"I didn't find anyone. But take a whiff of this," I said, handing him the wine bottle. "What do you smell?"

"Cheap wine," he said.

"Keep smelling," I insisted.

"There is something else here, a chemical of some kind."

"Exactly. **Something was added to that wine,** and I don't think it was Ovaltine," I said. "I think that one of those three characters drugged the other two so he could go and dig up the treasure by himself. But we still don't know where that treasure is."

"Oh, yes we do," said Longh. "Follow me." And so there I was, walking behind Longh down the cobblestone avenue toward the temple of the pyramid. As we moved farther in that direction, something around the altar caught my eye. It was a pile of loose stones. As I got closer I could see that the top of the altar was smashed into pieces.

Longh got there first. When I caught up with him, he simply pointed straight down the gaping hole that was now the top of the altar. I looked and saw an ancient stone stairway descending into some pitch-dark underground room. The dusty ground around the altar was full of footprints, half of them showing **two nails missing from the left heel.**

Longh got the flashlights, and we went down together. Farther down was a stone door, **blown to pieces by an explosion.** That, of course, was the "thunder" I had heard last night. When we stepped inside, I saw the spookiest sight I've ever seen.

There were row after row of human skeletons sitting on stone benches. Each was wearing some sort of warrior costume. And each held in his hand a silvery metal box. Strewn over the skeletons were smashed metal boxes they had probably been guarding long ago.

Longh and I looked at each other and said the same three words at the same time: "The golden wealth."

Spilling from each box were grains from some kind of plant.

"Where's the gold?" I asked Longh.

"I don't think we're going to find any," Longh said. "Do you know what this is, Dakota?" he said, pointing to the caskets. "Wheat. Golden wheat. The Lanerans did not have big farms. It was hard to grow food in the jungle, so when they had a good harvest they locked away their special strains of wheat as protection against a bad harvest. I will bet that when they thought their civilization was finished they gathered up all their wheat and entrusted it to their soldiers to guard for the rest of their lives. Not that they had a choice," he said, pointing toward the floor. Around both ankles of each skeleton was a steel shackle attached to a chain imbedded in the stone floor. "And here we have it," Longh said, reaching into one of the open caskets, "the golden wealth of Lanera: wheat."

"That's what the thief got. Stale wheat?" I couldn't stop laughing. Then I realized something.

The government orders. It was time to open that document Professor Bricknow had sent me. I opened the sealed envelope. Inside was one letter and another sealed envelope. The letter, addressed to Bricknow, was stamped TOP SECRET—OPEN ONLY WHEN GOLDEN TREASURE IS LOCATED.

TOP SECRET

Professor Bricknow
LELAND UNIVERSITY
135 Russell Mills Road
New Bedford, MA 02748

OPEN ONLY WHEN GOLDEN TREASURE IS LOCATED

ROCKET
RESEARCH
LABORATORY

2731 CROSSTIMBERS ROAD   HOUSTON, TX 77093

TO: Professor Bricknow
FROM: Rocket Research Lab, Special Projects
RE: Lanera

One of our agents believes that there is concealed with the golden treasure a special metal. Its properties are that it is lighter than any metal known and practically indestructible. We must have a sample of that for a special alloy we are making for rockets. Do what you want with the golden treasure, but we need the white metal.

I then opened the other envelope, addressed to me. Inside was a note from Professor Bricknow:

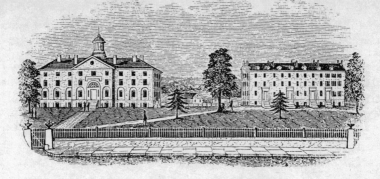

LELAND UNIVERSITY
135 RUSSELL MILLS ROAD   NEW BEDFORD, MA 02748

Dakota,

The fact that you are reading this means that you have found the golden treasure and the special metal in which it is stored. This metal is extremely rare, found only in a handful of places on earth. Years ago, as a young archaeologist, I had found a small chest made out of this metal, called nytonal. I showed it to a friend who is a government scientist, and ever since I have been looking for more of the same. I knew from my research that the golden treasure of Lanera was stored in this metal, considered sacred to the priests. But no one knew where that treasure was, and for years no one even had a clue of where to begin the search.

Now that you have found the metal, guard it with your life. It is worth more than a thousand times its weight in gold. It may even be worth more than the treasure itself.

Please destroy this note and the one that came with it when you have finished reading them.

Professor Bricknow

"Well, I'll be," I said, holding a cigarette lighter under the two sheets of paper. "Who would have thought these tin boxes were worth so much? That answers a lot of questions."

"True, but I have another," said Longh.

"What?"

"Where did everybody go?"

"Based on what we found, I think the thief was in the group we saw last night. Either Patchin, Ortega, or Dank is the guy who drugged the wine, the same way he drugged our food that first night. While the others were in a deep sleep the suspect cracked open the altar, which he located with the help of the medallion, **blew the door off the underground chamber with explosives,** and found himself with a roomful of skeletons and old wheat. After he found nothing but old wheat he left, and the others chased him as best they could. It's funny, after all that trouble the only thing he got for his trouble was the medallion."

"I wouldn't be too sure about that," said Longh, studying the rows of skeltons. "I count one hundred skeletons and only ninety-nine of these metal boxes. Whoever was here took one as a little souvenir. Who knows? Perhaps he thought it was worth something."

When we arrived back in Paramar, we stopped in a jungle village. There I met the remarkable young man who offered to deliver this to you, Boss, when he returned to college in the U.S.A. Because of the sacred nature of the material, he had to wear his native costume.

I happen to know our thief is going to try to sell the medallion to Professor Bricknow. You can probably snag the crook at the university or when he lands at the airport if you can figure out in time whom to arrest. Wish I could come and help, but **I'm outta here, Boss!**

From:
DAKOTA KING
DISAPPEARING INC.

To:
ZONE OPERATIONS ORGANIZATION
9909 INCOGNITO DRIVE
ARLINGTON, VIRGINIA 90909

And The Villain Is . . .

. . . ORTEGA

As I was thinking over our adventures, there were certain things that seemed to tie in with Mr. Ortega's background. The fact that he had once been a knife thrower as an entertainer automatically made me suspicious. He could have been disguised as one of those dancers in costume when he threw the knife at the cafe. I first began to suspect him the day he gave me his business card. The note he wrote closely matched the writing on the note wrapped around the knife handle. And don't forget his injury—the day after the medallion was stolen from the glass case he had a bandaged hand. That got my antenna up.

But throughout the adventure there was something nagging at me. Just about everything dangerous that happened to me and Longh seemed to involve drugs or chemicals. There was that chemical coating on the fruit in our room that attracted the spiders; there was the drugged food we ate on our trip with Miguel/Dank/Arturo; there were the drugs used to make those poison darts they were firing at us; there were drugs in the water that Longh drank and that someone knew enough about it to locate and hide that warning statue; and finally there was the drugged wine found at the camp. And then it came to me in a flash. I remembered

Ortega standing there pouring wine for the others the night before.

It all fit together. Ortega, if you'll remember, was a chemistry teacher and would by his training know a lot about drugs. And as a member of the Order of the Phoenix, he would know a lot about native lore. He would be able to make the poison darts, and he would know what that ugly statue by the waterhole meant. And don't forget he was the one who provided me and Longh with the food we ate that knocked us out.

But how did he find out about the volcano rumor? There was that two-way radio in his backpack. Ortega already impressed me with his efficient spy system the day we met, and he knew everything important there was to know about us. One of his spies intercepted Zan's message to me at the hotel, then contacted Ortega on the radio. That white clay I saw in his backpack, of course, was plastic explosives which he used to blow open the tomb. It would take someone handy in chemistry to handle that stuff.

Sorry I never did get to check out whether his boots had two nails missing. But I'll bet any amount of money those are his. Ortega knew a lot about me and Longh, as I said. He probably also knew that we were expert trackers and would see anything distinctive about any tracks he made. So whenever he planned anything that we might check out he would make himself limp by putting a stone in his shoe. That's why the boot prints were uneven.

Finally, Ortega was the one with the most reasons for trying to steal the treasure. Arturo or Dank, as we knew him, turned out to really be a government agent and wasn't likely to be the thief. Sure Patchin had been a thief, but that was only once and only when black-mailed. If he was going to steal the medallion, why didn't he do a more subtle job of it? He was in the museum with it every day. He could even have switched a fake medallion for it and no one would have found out for a long, long time.

No, Ortega was my man. He was convinced that his people—or at least he—deserved the treasure. And for a friendly guy he was pretty quick with a knife, as I found out the day I woke him up. And there was another thing bothering me: why did he carry around a plane schedule on a U.S. airline in his backpack unless he was going there as soon as he found the treasure, maybe to sell it to a rich American museum?

Well, all he has now is that gold medallion, a box made of funny metal, and a wild story to tell. But if he's as shrewd as I think he is, he's going to figure out there's something special about that metal box. He's bound to start wondering why anyone would send one of the world's top agents-at-large (that's me, Boss, in case you were wondering) to the middle of the jungle to look at boxes of wheat. Ortega is a chemist, and it is just a matter of time before he does a few tests on that tin box of his and realizes what he has.

What you or someone in the Z.O.O. have to do is get to him before he does that, or the secret behind our mission to the Haunted City of Gold will be a secret no more. So keep an eye out on all international airports, and when my buddy Ortega comes walking through, ask him if he got the heel fixed on his boot. The left one.

Dakota King

"I'm outta here, Boss!"

Congratulations!

You've solved the case of The Haunted City of Gold! But that doesn't mean you can quit yet. There are other files for you to dig into in The Secret Files of Dakota King series.

Now that you've proven yourself to be a case-cracker of the highest quality, you're ready to take on the other cases. You are requested to join the secret agents at Zone Operations Organization (also known as the Z.O.O.), and help them solve the unsolved cases left behind by that always-on-the-go, agent-at-large, Dakota King. King and Longh Gonh, his partner at Disappearing Inc., are off on yet another exciting adventure. The results of their travels are always the same—files full of clues, transcripts, maps, scraps of paper, sketches, photographs, and who knows what else. Are you ready to face the next case?

Get some rest and plenty of it (you deserve it after The Haunted City of Gold). Dakota King, Longh Gonh, the Zoo-keeper . . . They're all counting on YOU!